Sing

A Comedy about a Musical

by Rick Abbot

A SAMUEL FRENCH ACTING EDITION

SAMUEL FRENCH

FOUNDED 1830

NEW YORK HOLLYWOOD LONDON TORONTO

SAMUELFRENCH.COM

ISBN 978-0-573-69271-0   Printed in U.S.A.   #21163

MUSIC USE NOTE

IMPORTANT BILLING AND CREDIT REQUIREMENTS

IMPORTANT BILLING AND CREDIT REQUIREMENTS

All producers *of SING ON! must* give credit to the Author of the Play in all programs distributed in connection with performances of the Play, and in all instances in which the title of the Play appears for the purposes of advertising, publicizing or otherwise exploiting the Play and /or a production. The name of the Author *must* appear on a separate line on which no other name appears, immediately following the title and *must* appear in size of type not less than fifty percent of the size of the title type.

SPECIAL FOREWORD

Although *Sing On!* is a sequel to that perennially popular play *Play On!*, the author has taken great pains to create this show in such a fashion that groups who have *not* done *Play On!* (if there *are* any groups who have not done that incredibly ubiquitous comedy) can still perform the sequel with equanimity, in the secure certainty that the new show can "stand on its own feet" as a unique entity. However, your author recommends highly that your regular patrons, after enjoying this sequel, might end up with a somewhat "time-warped" feeling if the success of this sequel with them encourages you to *then* do the preceding play, and so it *might* be better to do them *in order* for the optimum audience-enjoyment. Still and all, the two shows will "work" just splendidly, no matter in *which* order you decide to do them. And yet—*developments* among the roles (such as the tentative blossoming of First Romance between Billy and Violet in the original play resulting in Happy Marriage between them by the time of the follow-up play) somehow—to your author's inclinations, at least—make doing the shows in their actual sequence-of-existence a bit more soul-satisfying and logical. But—suit yourself. If you want to do this show without ever having done its predecessor, go ahead. It will be no less hilarious.

Rick Abbot

CHARACTERS

GERALDINE "GERRY" DUNBAR, a community theatre director

AGGIE MANVILLE, a stage manager, prompter and pianist

LOUISE PEARY, a backstage maid-of-all-work

HENRY BENISH, a middle-aged actor, the spouse of

POLLY BENISH, a middle-aged actress on the plump side

MARLA "SMITTY" SMITH, an eager ingenue in her early twenties

SAUL WATSON, an almost-middle-aged actor

BILL CAREWE, an actor in his mid-twenties

VIOLET [nee IMBRY] CAREWE, Bill's wife

PHYLLIS MONTAGUE, a local amateur playwright

MONTE MONTAGUE, Phyllis's nephew, a hobbyist songwriter

TIME: The present
LOCALE: The stage of a community theatre

ACT I
A multi-scened montage of rehearsals

ACT II
Opening Night of the Montagues' co-created
musical

ACT I

Scene 1

SCENE: [NOTE: Because of the multiplicity of scenes in which the sets are slowly created and installed onstage, a Set-Design series *of drawings would be a bulky mess, so you will not find one in this script. But suffice it to say that the ultimate set will be a Throne Room of suitable majesty (casements, archways rather than doors, a centered royal throne on an imposing dais more-or-less upstage center, and shields, banners, spears, swords-and-the-like suitably arrayed on the various wall-spaces). The stunning magnificence, or woeful lack of it (thanks to "make-do" artifacts/construction) is entirely up to your personal inclination; the way this show turns out, nothing in the world could distract the audience from what's happening onstage.]*

AT RISE: We find the usual helter-skelter vista of a bare stage (a ladder here, a workbench there, a rack of costumes in need of dusting, etc.), with several folding chairs opened and raggedly lined in center-stage area to face the auditorium. POLLY and HENRY are seated near the center of this grouping, and GERRY is standing facing them from the general center-left area. We find them all in mid-discussion:

POLLY. Really, Gerry, can't you even give us a *hint* of some kind?

GERRY. I guess I *could*, Polly—but that would start a discussion, and I'd have to keep backtracking to Square One for each newcomer. I'd rather wait till *everyone's* arrived.

HENRY. But it's all so *mysterious*, Gerry. This time of year, there'd normally be an audition-call out for the new show—but there's been *nothing*. (*Turns to POLLY*.) Unless we got a flyer you forgot to tell me about?

POLLY. Have I *ever* neglected to keep you posted on *theatre*-doings, Henry?

HENRY (*Logically*.) How would I have any way of *knowing* if you had?

GERRY. Trust me, Henry, there *was* no flyer. This is a rather—*special* sort of show.

POLLY. Without *open* auditions? Why?

HENRY. Yes, we've never done a show with *pre*-casting of the roles ... is that what *this* is?

GERRY. Honestly—please—I'd rather wait until *everybody* gets here. Then, I promise—

POLLY. But how many are *coming*?

HENRY. And how long do you plan to *wait* for everybody?

POLLY. If there are any no-shows, we could be waiting here all night!

GERRY. Just a few more minutes. I'm sure they'll all come. I said eight o'clock, and it's just barely two minutes past, and the people I asked are usually punctual—(*Pauses, listening toward left*.) Oh, good, I think I hear somebody *now* ...

(*AGGIE enters L, stops*.)

AGGIE. Oh, good, you haven't told them yet.

HENRY. Why, Aggie, how could you possibly know that?

AGGIE. You're still *here*.

GERRY. Aggie, please, this is going to be tough enough, without—

POLLY. What is?

HENRY. This is worse than mysterious. It's starting to feel *ominous*.

GERRY. That's nonsense, Henry. Aggie, why don't you sit down and relax.

AGGIE. (*Has moved D near L proscenium, now lounges against it.*) Uh-uh. When they attack, I want to be on my feet near the exit.

POLLY. (*Stands.*) Now, really, Gerry, I must *insist* that you inform us why—(*Pauses as LOUISE enters L and remains just U of AGGIE.*)

LOUISE. Oh, good, she hasn't *told* you yet! I was afraid I'd miss all the fun.

HENRY. What fun, Louise? What is going *on* here?

LOUISE. I just want to see the expressions on your faces when Gerry drops her bombshell.

POLLY. Gerry, this isn't fair! If Aggie and Louise already know what's going on, why—?

GERRY. (*With an impatient scowl at the newcomers.*) Polly, it's not the same thing. Aggie and Louise work as *individuals* during a show. The cast is something else again. I want to tell our actors as a *group*.

HENRY. Polly, I think I understand what Gerry's getting at. Come on, sit down—(*She will do so, with some reluctance, as he finishes:*) —and let's wait for the others. It can't be anything really *dreadful* if Aggie and Louise are here. I mean, they *know* whatever it is, and they still showed up.

POLLY. (*Mostly mollified.*) I *suppose* you're right, dear.

GERRY. Of course he is. And as soon as the others—oh, here they are, now!

(SAUL and SMITTY enter L, stop, look from twosome at proscenium to twosome on chairs, then at GERRY.)

SAUL. Is there anything wrong?

SMITTY. Everybody seems so ... tense ...

GERRY. (*Waving them toward chairs.*) Don't be silly. Everything's fine, just fine. Polly and Henry are just imagining all kinds of dire things simply because I held off telling them why we're here.

SAUL. (*As he and SMITTY seat themselves.*) Then this isn't a *casting*-call? I figured, this being the middle of February, it was time to try out for the spring musical.

GERRY. Well, actually, it *is* the reason we're here, in a way ...

POLLY. If that's the case, why ever are you being so mysterious about it?

LOUISE. To put it gently—there's a kind of *glitch*.

HENRY. About the musical?

AGGIE. Not *exactly* a glitch, that might be putting it too strongly ...

GERRY. *No* it's not.

SAUL. What *is* it, we're going to do *The Wiz* and there'll be repercussions if we try doing it in blackface?

GERRY. (*Laughs shortly*.) I only wish it *were* as simple as that!

SMITTY. You mean we *are* doing it in blackface?

LOUISE. We're not *doing The Wiz*, Smitty.

HENRY. But how many other shows *need* players in blackface?

POLLY. (*Helpfully*.) Well, there's *The Green Pastures*—

GERRY. This has nothing to *do* with blackface!

SAUL. Okay, I give up. What *is* the dire problem besetting us, all unbeknownst?

POLLY. Yes, what?

HENRY. Tell us, Gerry!

SMITTY. I'm starting to get all nervous!

LOUISE. Maybe you'd better tell them, Gerry. We've at least got a quorum.

GERRY. Well ... uh ...?

SAUL. Quorum? Who *else* is coming?

GERRY. Just two more. Bill and Violet.

HENRY. *Who*?! You don't mean Billy Carewe and Violet Imbry?

POLLY. Henry, she's not "Imbry" any more since she married Billy.

SAUL. But I thought they moved out of town when Bill got transferred?

AGGIE. He was transferred back two weeks ago.

POLLY. Oh, how marvelous! Why, I haven't seen them since—since—?

HENRY. (*Chuckling in reminiscence*.) Since we did *Phyllis's* play! Remember?

SMITTY. (*A rueful groan*.) Who could forget?!

SAUL. Props that weren't there when they should be, telephones that didn't ring when they should, guns going off without warning—

SMITTY. And the *rewrites*! *That* was the *worst* part! Phyllis showing up with new scenes every day, almost until the show *opened*—!

HENRY. It's no *wonder* none of us could learn our lines properly!

POLLY. Still, we *did* pull it off! The reviews were *quite* gratifying!

SAUL. Only because the reviewers thought the show was *supposed* to be a comedy!

SMITTY. (*Shivers.*) Boy, I never want to go through anything like *that* again ...!

HENRY. Amen!

GERRY. Oh, dear. I was afraid of that.

(*The merriment of the seated group subsides immediately; each member of the group will come slowly to his/her feet as he/she speaks:*)

SAUL. Oh, now, wait a minute—

POLLY. Gerry, you surely don't mean—?

SMITTY. Didn't we all take a solemn *vow* that we'd never *again*—

HENRY. —never in a *million years*—!

LOUISE. Now, wait, it's not so bad as all that—

AGGIE. Sure, a few things went *wrong* last time out, but—

GERRY. We did practically *sellout* business!

SAUL. Holy hell! Then—it's *true*?!

SMITTY. A show by Phyllis Montague?!

POLLY. And it's a *musical*?!

HENRY. (*Starts off L.*) I'd better go warm up the car–!

GERRY. *Wait!* (*HENRY pauses short of exit.*) *Please* hear me out. *Then* make up your minds.

POLLY. (*Re-seating herself.*) Oh, come on, Henry. It's not like there's anything worth watching on *TV* tonight.

SAUL. Or *any* night!

(OTHERS laugh, and the mood brightens slightly; HENRY will move back to sit beside POLLY, and SAUL and SMITTY will sit again, during:)

GERRY. Oh, thank you! All of you!

AGGIE. (*Un-leans from proscenium.*) Well, if there's not going to be a lynching, I guess I *will* sit down! (*She and LOUISE find chairs and sit with OTHERS facing GERRY.*)

GERRY. The basic problem, see, is economics.

SAUL. Now, wait, that was the spiel you gave us *last* time we did a Phyllis Montague show. We were getting it royalty-free, and—

GERRY. It's *worse* than that, Saul, *this* time. We might—lose our theatre.

OTHERS. (*Various ad-libs of:*) Oh?/No kidding!/Is it *that* bad? [etc.]

GERRY. Business this season hasn't been exactly ... *brisk,* as you all well know. I think it's partly the national concern about spending money in tight times, combined with so many people preferring to stay *home* for entertainment on TV—

SAUL. Is *that* what they call it?!

GERRY. Anyhow, what it boils down to is that we've just been barely making the *rent* on this place, and our lease just came up for renewal and the rent has gone *up*, and—frankly—we *need* to do this musical. Bad.

SAUL. If *Phyllis* wrote it, I'm sure we *will* do it bad!

POLLY. Stop it, Saul! You *know* what Gerry means. But Gerry, seriously, if we're having box office problems *anyhow*, it seems to me that no matter *what* show we do—

GERRY. You didn't let me finish: *If* we do Phyllis's show ... we get a ten thousand dollar *endowment* for the theatre!

HENRY. I didn't know Phyllis Montague *had* ten thousand dollars!

AGGIE. She *hasn't!*

SAUL. Then *where*—?

LOUISE. If you'd clam up and let Gerry *finish*—!

SMITTY. Sorry, Gerry. Go ahead.

GERRY. Thank you. But just a minute—Louise, could you make us some coffee? I'm still shivering after the drive over here.

LOUISE. (*Will start slow stroll toward R wings.*) Sure enough. I guess I've seen all the funny facial expressions I'm going to. (*Will exit, at her own pace, sometime during:*)

AGGIE. Actually, it's kind of *warm indoors* here. I think my *overcoat* is what's causing the chill after being outside. (Will undo front of overcoat, but keep it on [*NOTE: Except for GERRY, the OTHERS are each garbed—buttoned-up or open—in some sort of winter outer garments].*)

GERRY. I think I took *mine* off too *soon*!

SMITTY. Why *did* you?

GERRY. Psychology, I guess. I thought that if *I* didn't look all bundled up and ready to leave, it might keep everyone *else* around till I'd explained matters.

POLLY. (*Delicately.*) Which you *still* haven't *done*, by the way ...

HENRY. Yes, Gerry—where is this ten thousand dollars *coming* from?

GERRY. Have you heard of an organization called "Bess Boosters"?

SAUL. Has *anybody*?

GERRY. (*Ruefully.*) I know what you mean! But the point is—*Phyllis* has, and they've commissioned *her* to *write* this show!

SAUL. A light begins to dawn! We do Phyllis's show, or we lose ten thousand bucks!

AGGIE. *And* our theatre, Saul.

SAUL. Oh boy. Talk about a rock-and-a-hard-place!

GERRY. Exactly. *However*—knowing how you all feel about the trauma from the *last* show of Phyllis's we did—

SMITTY. And we all prayed it *would* be the last show of hers we did!

GERRY.—I've made certain pre-arrangements with Phyllis. First of all, the script she submits will be the *only* script we're going to use. In other words, *no* rewrites!

POLLY. Well, *that* helps, quite a bit!

GERRY Secondly, I made her *swear* that she will *not* constantly *interrupt* when we're in rehearsals!

SAUL. You mean we might actually get through a scene without her offstage *screams*?

HENRY. It's sounding better all the time!

GERRY. And, *finally*, if we *have* to make certain adjustments for practical reasons, in any of her lines or stage business, she is to bow to *our* decision, and *not* threaten to take her show *elsewhere!*

SAUL. And she *agreed* to your terms?

GERRY. Amazingly enough—yes. Every one. And do you know *why...?*

SAUL. You were sitting on her chest at the time?

POLLY. Saul! Will you cut out being a cut-up?!

SAUL. How's that again?

POLLY. You know very well what I mean! Gerry, I just had a *marvelous* idea! Why don't we make a mandate that every time Saul interrupts with one of his dumb jokes, he has to pay a fine?

GERRY. Really, Polly—!

SAUL. Gerry, she's only saying that because *she's* almost always the *butt* of my jokes!

HENRY. (*Stands.*) Now, *stop* with the fat-jokes, Saul! It's not Polly's fault she's so—(*Stops short, trying to dredge up a polite term.*) —sort of on the *plump* side!

SAUL. *Sort* of? Henry, if Polly were a murder victim, the chalk-outline around her corpse would be a *circle!*

POLLY. There! Gerry, if we *do* fine Saul every time he says something like that, we'll get the ten thousand dollars from *him* by the end of the show!

GERRY. You know, you've got a *point* there ...

SAUL. Aw, Ger, can't a guy have a little fun? I *love* Polly! It's just that she lays herself *open* to teasing so well!

HENRY. But fat-jokes are unkind, Saul. Polly's weight isn't her fault. She has trouble with her *glands.*

SAUL. Yeah. Her *salivary* glands!

POLLY. That's *two!* What do you say, Gerry? We could make a fortune!

SMITTY. Hold it, *all* of you! We haven't *heard* everything yet. *I* want to know *why* Phyllis agreed to Gerry's terms—*without* Saul's interruptions!

SAUL. Actually, *I'd* like to know the reason, *myself* ...

GERRY. Pure and simple: Phyllis *adores* you people! She told me she'll always *treasure* you, because you all worked so *hard* to do her very first *play!*

HENRY. Gerry, *Phyllis* is the reason it *was* so hard!

LOUISE. (*Re-enters from R, stands there, near R wings.*) Coffee's perking.

GERRY. Good! Now, will you all please let me finish?

LOUISE. Who's *stopping* you?

GERRY. *Everybody*, you included!

LOUISE. *Wow*, what side of the bed did *you* get up on today?! (*Turns, not angrily, re-exits R, on:*) Show business is always such a lark!

GERRY. I'm sorry. I guess I *am* being a bit cranky. I've just been so keyed up with worry, wondering how you'd all *respond* to the situation—

POLLY. Well, we haven't walked out *yet*, have we?

SAUL. Relax, Gerry, you're among friends. Go on about this endowment-thing.

SMITTY. And *please* tell us why, with a zillion playwrights on the planet to choose from, this endowment-group selected *Phyllis* to write this show!

GERRY. The Bess Boosters is run by a committee. They'd already selected a *composer* for the show, and asked *him* to select the playwright. And the composer selected Phyllis because—

SAUL. —he's a nutcake?

OTHERS. SAUL!

SAUL. (*Cringing slightly.*) Sorry.

GERRY. The composer's name is "Monte *Montague*." Does *that* give you a clue?

POLLY. Oh, my.

SMITTY. Wouldn't you know!

HENRY. It's beginning to make sense.

SAUL. You mean we get to cope with *two* Montagues, Gerry? What sort of mandates have you laid on *him*?

GERRY. (*Uneasily.*) Well, actually, I haven't *met* the gentleman yet ...

AGGIE. Phyllis is bringing him by at eight-thirty.

SAUL. (*Looks at wristwatch.*) That gives us five minutes to run for our lives.

GERRY. Now, *stop* that, Saul! He *must* have talent, or the committee wouldn't have *selected* him!

SAUL. (*Reluctantly.*) Well ... I suppose *that's* a point in our favor ... What *is* he, some kind of *relative*?

GERRY. It's my understanding Monte is Phyllis's *nephew*—

SAUL.—who has *just* tiptoed out of the asylum—

POLLY. Now, Saul—!

SAUL. Polly, the man picked *Phyllis* to author his script! He *must* be a lunatic!

HENRY. Saul's got a point, dear.

SMITTY. Say, isn't that *nepotism*? I know it has *something* to do with hiring nephews.

AGGIE. Yeah, but he hired her, Smitty. That makes it—uh—"auntie-tism"? (*When OTHERS stare at her, she rises, on:*) I'll just go help Louise with the coffee. (*Will exit R during:*)

POLLY. What *I'd* like to know is—what in the world is a "Bess Booster"?

GERRY. Ah, that's the interesting part—

SAUL. Finally!

GERRY. You know, Saul, I might *take* Polly's suggestion about cut-up fines ...

SAUL. Oh, all right, all right! (*Slumps down a bit in his chair, arms folded, muttering:*) Bunch o'party-poopers...

GERRY. As I understand it from Phyllis, the Bess Boosters is a group of Anglophiles—

SMITTY. A group of *what*?

SAUL. And *you* a college-girl! Even *I* know *that* term!

SMITTY. Then it's probably something *dirty*!

GERRY. *Smitty*! I'm surprised at you! That kind of crack is more in *Saul's* line.

SAUL. I drive her to rehearsals. I must be contagious.

POLLY. Smitty, I thought you got your driver's license *years* ago!

'SMITTY. Oh, I did. The problem is, I can't afford college tuition *and* car payments!

HENRY. Could we get back to *our* economic problems?

GERRY. Thank you, Henry. Anyhow ... this is a group who delights in anything having to do with the *English*.

SAUL. (*To SMITTY.*) *That's* what an Anglophile is.

OTHERS. SAUL!

SAUL. Aw, c'mon, you *can't* fine me for being *instructive*!

GERRY. But we *might* for being *interruptive*!

SAUL. Okay-okay-okay! Onward, onward!

GERRY. Thank you. Now, this *particular* group finds its fascination in that part of British history centering around Queen Elizabeth the First, who was also known as "Good Queen Bess."

POLLY. But why do they call themselves Bess *Boosters?*

GERRY. Well, you see—

(But ALL now look off L as we hear a merry carol from:)

PHYLLIS. *(Off.) Yoo-hooo!* (*ALL EXCEPT SAUL stiffen in apprehension.*)

SAUL. Hark! It's the cry of The Feather-Headed Dramatist!

(OTHERS make hasty shushing-noises at him, and he subsides as PHYLLIS enters, with a gentle-looking little man, MONTE, in tow.)

PHYLLIS. *(Flutteringly, cooingly, expansively.)* Hello, hello, hello! Isn't this all simply *thrilling?!* Together again, after so *many-*many years! How have you all *been?*

SAUL. *(Genially.)* Healing nicely.

GERRY. *(Quickly.)* Phyllis, you timed your arrival perfectly! I was *just* about to explain to the group the *reason* those Bess Boosters *call* themselves that! *(With ill-concealed relief:)* Now *you* can do it! *(Will quickly move to group and take a seat.)*

PHYLLIS. Oh, Geraldine, I should be *delighted* to do so!... Ah, but I'm forgetting my manners! I should like all of you to meet my nephew, Monte, who will be doing the *songs* for our little show! *(Ad-lib murmur of Hi/Howdy/Pleased to meet you/etc. from group.)* And Monte—*(He will formally, almost shyly, nod/bow to each introducee in turn:)*—may I present Geraldine Dunbar, our delightful director ... (*LOUISE and AGGIE, with paper cups of coffee on a tray, will enter L at this juncture, and stop just onstage, listening.*) Polly Benish, my *special* friend and actress ... Henry Benish, her charming husband ... Marla Smith, a clever young player ... Saul Watson, a fine dramatic actor in *older* roles ...

SAUL. (*Restrains himself from a direct retort:*) You would *love* my "King Lear"!

MONTE. (*Erroneously impressed.*) Ah?

PHYLLIS. And those ladies with the refreshments are Agnes Manville, a simply *sterling* stage manager ... and Louise Peary, who—um—does something-or-other backstage! (*Delivers this last bit with a pretty little laugh of uncertainty.*)

LOUISE. (*Dryly.*) I keep the *mice* from migrating onstage.

MONTE. (*Genuinely surprised.*) Oh, dear, I didn't know this place was infested with *vermin*!

POLLY. Then you don't know *Saul!*

MONTE. Hmm?

SAUL. Point of order, Gerry! Does this fine-threat work *both* ways?

PHYLLIS. *What* threat...?

HENRY. It's just some in-joke stuff, Phyllis, dear. You *know* how our players like to tease one another!

MONTE. (*Relieved.*) Then there *aren't* any mice—?

GERRY. No-no-no, of course not! Louise is our *tech* person—handles lights, sound-effects, like that.

MONTE. (*To LOUISE.*) You don't mean—manually?

LOUISE. Well, see, I *tried* running the lightboard with my *toes*, but—

GERRY. Louise, *please*...?

MONTE. (*To PHYLLIS, uneasily.*) With her *toes*, Aunt Phyllis?

PHYLLIS. Now-now, Louise was just having her little joke—(*To LOUISE.*) —I *presume...?*

MONTE. But that's so *backward*—!

POLLY. Monte, it was a joke, she *doesn't* run the tech with her toes!

MONTE. Oh, I don't mean that. I mean, even doing it *manually* is so out-of-step these days. In the modern theatre, all that stuff is handled by *computer!*

LOUISE. Gosh-a-mighty, I *am* an oaf! That's what I get for falling off the turnip truck!

GERRY. Louise, will you please pass out the coffee, and *listen* to what Monte's saying?

LOUISE. (*As she and AGGIE start handing out coffee to everybody.*) May as well. But it's kind of sad slipping from theatre technician to waitress!

MONTE. Oh, dear, I haven't made myself clear. I wasn't *firing* you or anything, Louise. I was just suggesting we *get* a computer for the theatre-tech; *you* could be the one *running* it, of course.

GERRY. *Get* one?! Monte, those things cost *money!*

PHYLLIS. But surely, Geraldine, your theatre group *has* money—?

GERRY. (*Almost Telling All.*) If we *had*, would we be doing *your* stup—(*Catches herself, changes words with only a millisecond's hesitation:*)—pendous show in such a *tiny* theatre?!

SAUL. (*Admiringly, blurts:*) Gerry, that's what *I* call a *save!* (*As she glares at him, he corrects swiftly to PHYLLIS.*) The *money*, I mean. The *money* we save. By

having a—um—small theatre. Is what I mean. Meant.
About the—

POLLY. (*Before he completely submerges.*) Phyllis,
please tell us about the show!

HENRY. Yes, we're all fascinated by the project.

SMITTY. Especially why the Bess Boosters *call*
themselves that!

PHYLLIS. (*As any author, is distracted by this from
SAUL's fumbling.*) Oh, it's devastatingly delightful. You
see, when Queen Elizabeth reigned, she was, alas, *much*
maligned.

SMITTY. Much *what?*

GERRY. She got a lot of Bad Press.

SMITTY. Oh.

SAUL. But didn't she *deserve* it? I mean, anybody who
disagreed with her got their *heads* lopped off!

MONTE. Rumors! Ugly rumors! The very sort of
rumors that the Bess Boosters was founded in order to set
right!

AGGIE. I'm getting a glimmering. What they're trying
to boost is the queen's *reputation?*

PHYLLIS. Exactly, Agatha! So many terrible things
were said about her—it is the purpose of my little show to
correct all those unfortunate errors!

LOUISE. But how can you correct historical *fact,*
Phyllis? I mean, for instance, we all *know* she ordered
Mary, Queen of Scots, put to *death. That* wasn't very nice.

PHYLLIS. Ah, but that was all a mistake! She was put
to death by *accident!*

SMITTY. What *kind* of accident?

PHYLLIS. Well, Mary *was* Scottish, you know, and
one day Elizabeth, who much admired Mary's clothes,

happened to say, "You know, I'd *love* to have her *kilt!* " Well, the palace executioner happened to overhear her, and he misunderstood, and—

SAUL. Phyllis. Is *that* one of the details that comes up in your script?

PHYLLIS. Naturally!

SAUL. The script you've promised *not* to alter?

PHYLLIS. Yes, of course. I gave Geraldine my solemn *vow* that the scripts I am going to pass out to you tonight are to be performed *precisely* as they are now written, and I am *not* going to change a single solitary *word!*

(ALL sit frozen for about one second; then:)

SAUL. *(Abruptly leans forward, hands clasped to his chest, on:)* Even if we *beg?!*

GERRY. *(Before PHYLLIS can quite figure this out.)* Say, now, where *are* those scripts, *anyhow?!*

PHYLLIS. Oh, dear, I believe I left them in the car! Monte, would you—?

MONTE. *(Turns and heads L.)* Of course, Auntie Phyllis! *(Exits.)*

PHYLLIS. Are there any other questions while we're waiting?

SMITTY. Yes. Who plays who?

SAUL/POLLY/HENRY. *(In actor-eagerness unison:)* Yeah!

PHYLLIS. Well, I thought Polly could play Mary, Queen of Scots—

SAUL. *(Despite himself.)* You're going to cover *that* in *plaid?!*

HENRY. Never mind him, Phyllis. Please go on.

PHYLLIS. And the *key* role, that of Elizabeth *herself,* should be played by a *young* girl. (*SMITTY starts to preen.*) Someone fresh ... vital ... ravishingly beautiful ...

LOUISE. I thought the queen was totally *bald!*

SMITTY. "Bald"?!

LOUISE. *Totally.* Didn't even have *eyebrows!*

SAUL. Thus originating the courtly question, "What *have* you done with your *hair*?"!

PHYLLIS. Do you know—I'll bet you're *right!*

SAUL. You *do*?!

SMITTY. But I thought this was going to be a *romantic* role ...

PHYLLIS. Oh, it's *very* romantic. Consider, for instance, her passionate love affair with Lord Essex! Poor woman. So sad that he died before the two of them could wed.

GERRY. Phyllis, she had him *beheaded!*

PHYLLIS. She did?!

POLLY. That's the way *I* remember it!

SAUL. And *she* was an eyewitness!

POLLY. I *read* it in a *book!*

PHYLLIS. A *false* book! The very kind of book the Bess Boosters are trying to stamp out! And if I can *help* them to do so—

HENRY Ah! It's all coming together! *We* get the grant, and *you* get—?

PHYLLIS. Elected to the Bess Boosters Society! It's *very* exclusive, you know! That's why I was so *thrilled* when Monte told me—(*Stops as MONTE re-enters L with armload of scripts.*) But we're wasting precious time! *Wait* until you see what I've done! Monte—?

MONTE. Of course. Immediately. (*He will pass out scripts to ALL except PHYLLIS, during:*)

SAUL. But just how exactly does this thing *work*, Phyllis? We *do* the show, and you send them a note saying we've *done* it? Or—?

PHYLLIS. Oh, they're *much* more careful than *that*, Saul, otherwise *anybody* could *claim* to have boosted Good Queen Bess, after all! No, we'll have to have *proof*, of course.

GERRY. What proof? Theatre programs?

HENRY. Newspaper write-ups?

POLLY. Reviews?

SMITTY. Notarized affidavits?

AGGIE. Maybe a copy of the script?

PHYLLIS. Agatha, they've already *seen* the script!

MONTE. (*Almost through passing scripts out.*) *And* given it their enthusiastic approval, besides!

LOUISE. So what's *left*?

PHYLLIS. They want to *see* the show, of course!

SAUL. One tiny question: Do we get that ten thousand bucks *before* they see the show, or *afterwards*...?

MONTE. Oh, *before*, of course. What the money is for, in effect, is *payment* to you for putting it on! (*OTHERS EXCEPT PHYLLIS sit back and smile, with soft sighs of relief.*) If you agree to do it, once you've read the script, the money will be wired to your theatre *immediately*!

(*As if by Group Telepathy, the selfsame notion has crossed through the minds of all the little theatre group, and without realizing they look almost choreographed, each in turn rises to his/her feet [unless already standing, of course] on each line:*)

GERRY. Bah!

HENRY. What need to read?

POLLY. If this play is by Phyllis Montague—

SMITTY.—then it *has* to be worth our interest!

SAUL. But then, there never *was* a playwright quite like *you*, Phyllis!

PHYLLIS. (*Ecstatic.*) Why, Saul! I'm *profoundly* grateful!

SAUL. (*Claps a hand atop her shoulder, fondly.*) *Not* as grateful as the Dramatists Guild!

(Luckily, she takes this as a compliment, and simpers prettily.)

MONTE. Then you'll *do* the play, sight unseen?

LOUISE. It'd help if they *read** it before doing it.

AGGIE. Makes rehearsing so much easier.

PHYLLIS. Oh, and, Agatha—Louise—? You'll be delighted to know that the *setting* of the show should be almost *effortless* to construct!

GERRY. Just *one* setting? For a *musical*?

SAUL. Say, that *is* a break!

SMITTY. What *is* this set, Phyllis?

PHYLLIS. It's just a single room, Marla. Building the set should be utter simplicity!

LOUISE. Now, that's more like it!

AGGIE. What kind of room did you have in mind?

PHYLLIS. (*Rapturously.*) The Throne Room at Buckingham Palace!

---

*Past tense: "red," not "reed."

SAUL. (*As the jaws of AGGIE and LOUISE drop in horrified unison.*) Look on the bright side: You'll only need one chair!

POLLY. But Phyllis—do you think a *musical* is the proper format for *this* sort of saga?

PHYLLIS. Why *not*? Elizabeth's *father* was a songwriter!

LOUISE. Henry the Eighth?! What did *he* write?

MONTE. *Greensleeves,* among others.

AGGIE. *I* didn't know that!

HENRY. (*Who's been paging through his script.*) Phyllis—what's a *scop*?

PHYLLIS. Oh, that's a sort of medieval minstrel, Henry.

SMITTY. (*Similarly.*) Hey, *here's* a weird one! Anybody know what an *estoc* is?

MONTE. That's a sort of hand-weapon from the Middle Ages—something like a sword.

POLLY. (*Similarly.*) Here's *another* stumper! What in the world is a *baldric*?

PHYLLIS. Let me think ... ah! That's a kind of *belt* they used to wear, when knights were bold, in order to have someplace to carry their weapons!

GERRY. (*Very uneasy.*) Phyllis, are you sure you should be using words the audience isn't likely to be *familiar* with? I mean, how will they know what the people are *talking* about?

PHYLLIS. Oh, I'm certain that anyone of intelligence will be able to figure the words out from their *context.* The meaning should be *perfectly* plain!

SAUL. (*Glumly.*) Yeah, about as plain as the *estoc* in a *scop*'s *baldric*!

MONTE. (*Slaps SAUL amiably on the back.*) There! I *knew* you'd catch on swiftly! (*SAUL just stares at him.*)

PHYLLIS. Besides, Geraldine, I'm *certain* the Bess Boosters will have *no* trouble understanding the language of the times, so where's the problem?

GERRY. Your theory is fine for the performance *they* attend, but what about all our *regular* customers at *subsequent* performances?

MONTE. You mean you'll be doing the show more than *once*?

AGGIE. We *have* to! That ten thousand bucks isn't going to last *forever*, you know!

SAUL. And business has been sparse *enough* lately without our alienating our patrons even *further*!

POLLY. We might lose our patrons to *other* theatres!

HENRY. Even to *television*!

MONTE. But I'm not sure I could stay *on* for an *extended* run of the show ...

SMITTY. You wouldn't *have* to, Monte. Matter of fact, once you turn your songs over to us, you could turn right around and go home *tonight*!

MONTE. But—I'm the *music* director!

GERRY. You are?!

PHYLLIS. That's why the Bess Boosters paid his way *here*, Geraldine. Otherwise, he could have simply *mailed* the score to you.

AGGIE. What's all the fuss about? Once Monte *has* musically-directed the show, there's no *need* for him to stick around.

PHYLLIS. But *Monte* is playing the Spanish Ambassador!

MONTE. (*Aghast.*) I *am*?

PHYLLIS. You won't be directing music *all* the time, dear! Now, don't pout! After all, if *Geraldine* is going to direct the *acting* part, and *she* doesn't mind playing a part, besides—

GERRY. *Whoa,* Nelly! Who *says* I don't mind?

PHYLLIS. But my dear, you *must*! The queen needs *all* the ladies-in-waiting possible, and I *truly* don't want my script in the hands of *strangers*! I was free to select *any* theatre company to do this show—but you all were so *splendid* about doing my *first* play that I couldn't *dream* of letting that endowment go elsewhere! Because, in case I never mentioned it before—I *love* you, one and all, so *very* much...!

SAUL. (*Helplessly abashed.*) Boy, talk about a *guilt* trip!

MONTE. I suppose I *could* look Spanish with the proper makeup ...

GERRY. And a lady-in-waiting doesn't have *too* many lines, I'd imagine ...

PHYLLIS. Oh, good! Then it's settled!

GERRY. Not quite! Phyllis, those *scops* and *baldrics* have *got* to go!

PHYLLIS. But you made me give my solemn word I *wouldn't* do rewrites...?!

GERRY. (*Gently.*) Phyllis, there's no problem with your fixing the script at the *start* of rehearsals.

POLLY. What bugged us *last* time was that you were still rewriting the play all the way up to dress rehearsal!

LOUISE. Not to mention the fact that the Middle Ages were over *long* before Elizabeth took the throne. She probably never saw a single *scop* in her *life!*

SAUL. (*Who's been leafing curiously through his script.*) Hey, what's this bit about William Shakespeare's knighthood?

HENRY. I didn't know he'd *been* knighted—you never hear "*Sir* William Shakespeare ..."

SMITTY. It *is* kind of *odd*, come to think of it. He was a favorite at court, and Elizabeth kind of *liked* him. Why *didn't* he ever get knighted?

AGGIE. Maybe he flunked out of Knight School!

GERRY. It *is* a mystery, that's for sure!

SAUL. (*Taps script.*) Not any *more*! Phyllis has *solved* the mystery *beautifully*! Nice job, Phyl!

HENRY. Which one of us *plays* Shakespeare?

SAUL. *I* do!

POLLY. No *wonder* Saul was so enthused!

SAUL. Though it seems to be a rather *short* part ...

PHYLLIS. Oh, don't worry about *that,* Saul, you're *also* playing Sir Walter Raleigh!

SAUL. (*Elated.*) *Really*?

SMITTY No, *Raleigh*!

MONTE. (*Moves over to her.*) I *like* a girl with a sense of humor!

LOUISE. *That* was *humor*?

SAUL. (*Who's been looking in script again.*) Hold it! Phyllis, how can I play Raleigh when he makes his entrance right after *Shakespeare* exits?

PHYLLIS. It's a *very* simple device, Saul. As Shakespeare, you wear a high-forehead *wig,* with longish hair hanging down in back, whereas as *Raleigh,* you wear an elegant long *cloak*, and a jaunty cap with a large feathered plume. All you have to do is step offstage, whip off the wig, don the hat and cloak, and come right on again.

SAUL. Well, I *guess* it could be managed ... I'll have to work on it.

GERRY. *Speaking* of work, I think we should all do a read-through of the play, right away.

POLLY. *Great* idea! And I especially want to hear my *songs!*

HENRY. That reminds me—I can carry a *tune* all right, but as for being a good *singer* ...

PHYLLIS. Now-now, don't worry about that, *any* of you! Just learn the lyrics, and the sheer *pageantry* will take care of the rest. After all, there's no reason to suppose the *Elizabethans* were particularly good singers, so—

MONTE. Oh, Auntie Phyllis, I seem to have one script left over, the one for Lord Essex.

PHYLLIS. Only *one?* You should have *two.* I counted them *most* carefully. One for Lord Essex, and another for *Elizabeth—*

SMITTY. (*Waves script.*) I've already *got* it, Phyllis, see?

PHYLLIS. Ah, *there's* the mistake! (*Takes script back from a shattered SMITTY.*) You don't *need* a *script.* You'll be playing a non-speaking part.

SMITTY. *What?* But—you said the Queen of England should be played by somebody *young*—fresh—vital—who *else* could do the part?!

PHYLLIS. Why ... *Violet,* of course! She was so *devastating* as Lady Diana in my *first* play! One could have *sworn* she was of royal blood!

SMITTY. That was a *part*! *I* could've looked royal if you hadn't had me playing the *maid!* Just what *do* I play in this show?!

PHYLLIS. A very *elegant* part, Marla. You will be one of the queen's ladies-in-waiting!

SAUL. That's Elizabethan for "maid"!

SMITTY. Of all the rotten—!

PHYLLIS. (*Hugs script to her breast.*) My decision is *final*, Marla! There is *no* way you could *possibly* play a queen!

MONTE. By the way, where *is* this Violet you told me about?

GERRY. She and Bill are on their way, I'm sure. Bill had to work a little late, tonight, but he promised they'd be here before nine.

SAUL. (*Consults wristwatch.*) It's almost that, now.

BILL. (*Off.*) Hello! Anybody *here?*

PHYLLIS. Ah, they've arrived! (*To SMITTY.*) And that's another thing, Marla—since Billy and Violet have *wed*, in *real* life, I've naturally assigned *him* the role of Lord Essex!

MONTE. That's this *last* script I've got.

SMITTY. But I'm *sure*, if you'd just let me *try* for the part, that I could convince you—

PHYLLIS. I'm sorry, but *no*, Marla! There is no *possible* way I could permit such a *vital* role to pass into unqualified hands! Violet is the *only* one I would entrust ·vith the part of the renowned Virgin Queen of England!

(Then BILL and VIOLET enter, L, and stop; VIOLET is obviously at least ten months pregnant.)

BILL. Hi there, everybody!

(There is a silence; then PHYLLIS sags, turns to SMITTY, and hands her the script; and as SMITTY clutches it to her heart in triumph—)

BLACKOUT

End of Scene 1

[NOTE: The longest any blackout in this show should last is five seconds, tops. Don't worry; blocking and costuming, etc., have all been taken into consideration so that your players should have no trouble being in their new spots (or offstage, as the occasion demands) by the time the lights come up full again. What we are going for, here, is a montage effect as one swift scene follows another, so that the passage of time will be conveyed to the audience without frazzling the cast. Five seconds is ample time for your players to step on or off the stage, don or doff a garment, move or remove a chair, etc., in time for lights-up. Trust me.]

ACT I

Scene 2

SCENE: During blackout, overcoats and other outer-wear have gone offstage, and won't be seen again unless specified. Players will be in their casual clothing for rehearsals (except when trying costumes, of course), but MONTE and PHYLLIS will look fairly dressy almost all the time. Chairs have been slightly shifted; they're all onstage, still, but one is in a Stage Center position (representing the throne), and the rest are off to one side and the other, as seating for onlookers who are not in whatever portion of the play is being rehearsed.

AT RISE: SMITTY is seated on center chair, BILL stands just to her right, facing her, PHYLLIS is standing to her left and slightly behind her, in a passing-on-vital-info pose, and SAUL is lounging on one of the chairs LC, legs stretched out, arms folded, observing. It is still early in rehearsals, so the performers, GERRY, and AGGIE, will usually have a script in hand or at least handy. Right now, SMITTY's script is open in her lap, and PHYLLIS is pointing out a passage.

PHYLLIS. Now, Marla, pay *close* attention! This is the lovely little scene where Lord Essex, trying to patch up their differences, and to allay Elizabeth's anger, gives her a little *pot*—

SAUL. I'll bet *that* mellows her out!

PHYLLIS. (*Straightens, gives him icy stare, and, as AGGIE strolls on from L:*) I am *talking* about the pot in which he has grown this lovely little *gillyflower!*

AGGIE. Hey, that reminds me, Phyllis. What *is* a gillyflower, and—more importantly—where can I *get* one?

BILL. Wouldn't *any* flower do?

AGGIE. Not a *Rafflesia!*

SMITTY. Why not?

AGGIE. The blossom's three feet across and the petals are one inch thick.

SMITTY. A *rose* would be nice. I think roses are romantic.

PHYLLIS. Oh, no, we mustn't chance that. The British used to fight *battles* over roses, the Lancasters versus the Yorks, one red, one white, and I'm not sure which faction Elizabeth favored.

SAUL. It'd hardly raise a *ruckus*, Phyllis. And it's nowhere *near* as bad as putting Elizabeth in the wrong throne room! I mean, *you* had her in Buckingham Palace a century before it was *built!*

AGGIE. (*Shrugs.*) Hardly a big deal, Saul. We just change the program to read *"Windsor Castle"* and we're home free.

PHYLLIS. I trust, Agatha, that you and Louise made the necessary readjustments in your plans for the stage setting?

AGGIE. (*Of course they didn't, but why make waves?*) Uh. Oh. Yeah, sure, sure, Phyllis. No problem. But before I start building it—(*Starts L.*)—*I've* got to use the *bathroom!*

SAUL. You'll have to wait your *turn ...*

AGGIE. (*Halts.*) Is *Violet* in there *again?*

SAUL. Well, Violet's been *eating* for two, and *drinking* for two, so it stands to reason, right *now* (*GERRY strolls on from L during:*) Violet's probably—

GERRY. Saul!

PHYLLIS. Probably *what?*

SAUL. Never mind.

BILL. Phyllis, can't Smitty and I just get *on* with the scene?

PHYLLIS. But knowing the *subtext* of what you're doing is *so* important!

GERRY. Phyllis, are you coaching *again*? I thought we decided *Violet* would do that?

PHYLLIS. But Violet's in the ladies room.

AGGIE. (*A small groan to GERRY.*) *Again*!

SAUL. We should build a couple more—we could have Men's, Women's and Violet's!

GERRY. (*Sternly.*) Saul, I suppose, from your merry banter, that you've learned *all* your lines?

SAUL. (*Straightens up in chair, fast.*) Uh, not quite, no. (*Quickly opens his script.*) But I'll get them, I'll get them.

GERRY. See that you do.

PHYLLIS. Geraldine, as long as time is of the essence, don't you think I might *continue*, at least till Violet returns?

GERRY. Oh ... I guess it can't do any harm.

PHYLLIS. Oh, good! Now, Marla, where were we?

SMITTY. Talking about that flower-thing. But I have a question.

PHYLLIS. Yes, dear?

SMITTY. If Elizabeth wasn't a Lancaster or a York, what *was* she?

PHYLLIS. A *Tudor!*

SMITTY. You mean, like a *sedan*?

SAUL. You're thinking of The Hatchback of Notre Dame!

GERRY. (*Warningly.*) Saulllll ...

SAUL. (*Buries head in script again.*) I'm *learning*, I'm *learning*!

BILL. Say, Phyllis, *I* have a question—isn't a potted plant as a gift for a *queen* kind of—oh—*chintzy*?

PHYLLIS. You must understand, William, that at this particular period of history, Queen Elizabeth was probably the wealthiest woman in the world. She had gold, silver, jewelry, costly gowns. So what *Essex* wanted to do was give her something that he was sure she *didn't* have, like a simple *flower*—

SAUL. Or a bottle of *hair*-restorer!

OTHERS. SAUL!

SAUL. Oh, okay, okay! (*Glumly returns to his script-studying as VIOLET enters from L.*)

AGGIE. *Finally!* (*Will half-gallop across and off L.*)

VIOLET. (*Strolling toward GERRY.*) How's Louise doing with the computer?

GERRY. (*Thumbs back R over her shoulder.*) Monte's explaining it to her. It's pretty tricky.

VIOLET. Darn nice of him to get us that loaner for the run of the show.

GERRY. Yeah, but I hope it doesn't *spoil* us, when we have to go back to *manual* tech.

VIOLET. (*By now has halted with GERRY in RC area.*) I doubt it. I don't completely *trust* computers.

GERRY. Who does? They're fast, but they're stupid.

PHYLLIS. Excuse me—I don't like to interrupt, but—should I go *on* while you're chatting, or is Violet ready to take over as coach?

VIOLET. I'm not sure. I mean, I can help people with their *lines* all right, but all this historical *background* is a complete *mystery* to me!

SMITTY. Same here!

PHYLLIS. But Marla, don't you know *anything* about those glorious days when England first became the "Mistress of the Seas"?

SMITTY. I suppose I would if I was majoring in history—but I wanted to major in math.

SAUL. (*Shrugs.*) Go figure! (*Then instantly, even as GERRY starts to open her mouth.*) I'm studying, okay? Guy's got to take a break *once* in a while...!

BILL. Look, can we cut all the discussion and *rehearse*? I've gotta get up for *work* in the morning!

SMITTY. It never bothered you when you were in *school*, Bill. You used to rehearse till *all* hours.

BILL. Smitty, I didn't get *paid* for going to school! And I've got a *wife* to support, and a *baby* on the way, and if I try napping in the *office* like I used to do in class—!

GERRY. Bill's right, let's get this thing moving! (*Opens her script.*) Where are we at?

BILL. That flower-bit.

PHYLLIS. (*Still hovering over SMITTY.*) Now, as we go along, I'll try to *explain* to you the *significance* of—

SMITTY. (*To GERRY, desperately.*) Does she *have* to?

GERRY. Phyllis, please, *not* while we're trying to get the scene run, okay—?

PHYLLIS. Certainly, Gerry. I'll just go and see if I can assist Monte and Louise! (*Trots off L and doesn't hear:*)

SAUL. Heaven help them.

GERRY. (*Too much in agreement to pounce on him.*) You can say *that* again! (*As he opens his mouth:*) But *don't!* ... Now, come on, guys, let's get this scene done!

BILL. Where from?

GERRY. (*Scanning script.*) Uh ... your entrance. Good a spot as any.

BILL. Right! (*Looks about uncertainly.*) Where's the *door*, anyhow?

GERRY. Let me think—Aggie showed me the sketch of the set—ah! *I* remember. Roughly upstage right. (*As BILL moves to that point and then turns:*) I don't suppose either of you can do this thing *off book*—? (*When SMITTY and BILL just stare at her:*) No, I didn't think so. Okay, get set—go!

BILL. (*Gets into character, then moves down till he's R of throne.*) "Gracious Majesty—!"

GERRY. Hold it!

BILL. Already?!

GERRY. Bill, this is the land's reigning monarch! It's customary—if you valued your *life* in those days—to move down in *front* of the throne and drop down on one *knee!*

BILL. But that'll put my *back* to the audience!

SAUL. Maybe more than *that* when you genuflect in *tights!*

GERRY. (*Gently but seriously.*) Shut up, Saul. Bill, you can turn your profile to the audience *after* you make your obeisance!

SMITTY. His *what?*

GERRY. Sorry. That was a Phyllis-word. I've got to stop *listening* to that woman! I mean, after you genuflect.

BILL. But won't that look awkward? From an *actor's* point of view—

SAUL. *You*?!

GERRY. Saul—!

SAUL. Aw, c'mon, Ger, I can't study lines with all this *gabbing* going on, *can* I?

BILL. Maybe if we *raked* the throne a bit, sort of angled it to face downstage right, then I could do the genuflection and *still* be seen—

SAUL. Sounds okay to *me*, Ger.

VIOLET. Me, too.

SAUL. About *time* you spoke up, Vi. I was beginning to think you were in a coma.

VIOLET. The baby was kicking.

GERRY. But we *can't* rake the throne, for two very good reasons: First, Louise and Aggie are already building the *throne room*, and if we move the *throne*, they'll have to re-design the *walls*!

BILL. Oh.

VIOLET. What's the *other* reason?

GERRY. Acoustics. We have to have the *piano* onstage, if we want the audience to *hear* it, and the dais for the throne's the only item big enough to *hide* it! If we rake it, the audience will see *Aggie*, sheet music and all!

SAUL. Hey, wait a minute! (*Stands, sets script aside.*) If Aggie's out *here*, *with* us, playing the piano, who are we using for *prompter*?

GERRY. It's *all* been worked out, Saul. She'll have her *script* with her, *too*, right on the music rack. Matter of fact, she says prompting from the *middle* of the stage is a *damn* sight easier than trying to whisper cues and lines from the *wings*!

BILL. Excuse me—

GERRY. What?

BILL. Could we *please* get this stupid *rehearsal* going?!

(*PHYLLIS reenters from R, during:*)

GERRY. Yes, yes, of course! Why don't you go back to your entrance-position, and—

PHYLLIS. But are you *certain* you have all the *nuances* straight?

BILL. (*Moving to position.*) Can't we run it with *crooked* nuances? It's *only* a *rehearsal*!

GERRY. Bill's right, Phyllis. Let's *block* the thing first, *then* do the polishing!

PHYLLIS. I *just* wanted them in the proper *mood,* Geraldine, with Lord Essex staunchly concealing his *rage*—

BILL. *Boy,* am I in the proper mood!

PHYLLIS. —and Elizabeth numbly facing the prospect of a long and lonely reign!

SMITTY. By the way, how long *did* Elizabeth reign?

BILL. (*Losing it.*) *Forty days and forty nights!*

VIOLET. Bill, darling, *please* don't lose your temper, the *baby* will hear! (*Starts moving off R, speaking gently toward her protrusion:*) Daddy didn't mean it, dearest. He was just play-acting! (*As she exits:*)

BILL. (*Shouts after her:*) Around *here*?! Fat chance!

GERRY. All right, all right! Let's get *on* with it! Places! Begin!

BILL. (*Same business, except that now he genuflects D of SMITTY, on:*) "Gracious Majesty—!"

AGGIE. (*Steps onstage from L, hollers across toward R wings:*) *Louise*! The *piano's* here!

BILL. (*Slams his script down, stands, during:*) Ohhhh—*damn* it!

LOUISE. (*Off R.*) Hallelujah! (*Will enter, trailed by MONTE, and cross toward AGGIE, on:*) Now maybe Monte will leave me *alone* to learn that control-board! (*She will exit L, AGGIE joining her, during:*)

SAUL. Come on, Bill, they could probably use a hand ... (*Exits L after duo.*)

BILL. (*Following him.*) May as well! It'll be nice to get *something* accomplished tonight!

SMITTY. (*Stands, rubs her posterior.*) I hope the real throne's more comfortable than *this*! I can't rule the British Empire from a metal folding-chair!

PHYLLIS. Oh, of *course* it is, dear! Absolutely *stunning* padded velvet on the arms and back!

SMITTY. (*Still rubbing.*) It's not my arms and back I'm *concerned* about! (*Will pick up BILL's flung-down script, during:*)

SAUL. (*Off L.*) We should have had *Polly* play the queen. *She* comes with her *own* padding! (*Then he emerges, along with LOUISE, AGGIE and BILL, rolling a small spinet onstage by group effort; it will end up with its back against center chair over the next several speeches.*)

PHYLLIS. Oh, that reminds me—how *are* dear Polly and Henry, Geraldine?

GERRY. Still fighting their head-colds. I *told* them not to sit around here all night in their overcoats. With the air below *zero* outside, when they went back out all *sweaty*—

MONTE. At least we can work *around* them for the time being ...

SAUL. Maybe around *Henry*—!

GERRY. Saul—!

BILL. Aw, c'mon, Gerry, you can't fine him for wisecracking when Polly's not *here!*

AGGIE. (*As piano moves into position.*) Right about *here* okay, Monte?

MONTE. Yes, that will do marvelously, Aggie!

VIOLET. (*Enters from R.*) Isn't that kind of beat-up for a royal throne room?

AGGIE. Nobody has to look at it but me.

MONTE. But where's the *bench?*

LOUISE. (*Heading L.*) Monte, give us a *chance,* for pete's sake! One thing at a time! (*Exits.*)

SMITTY. (*Dubiously.*) If the dais has to hide *this,* how high will that *throne* be?

AGGIE. *Please* don't tell me you're afraid of *heights!*

SMITTY. Oh, no, of course not, not in *that* way—

GERRY. Then in *what* way?

SMITTY. I was thinking of the *heat*—from the overhead *lights,* I mean. I'll be wearing a heavy gown, and that curly wig, and the nearer I get to those *lights,* the *hotter* it will get!

SAUL. Don't worry, the *velvet* will soak up the sweat!

LOUISE. (*Reenters toting small piano bench.*) Here you go, Aggie. See if this thing fits your behind! (*Will pace it in proper position U of piano, during:*)

AGGIE. I think *Monte* should have the honor. I'm *dying* to hear the *score* of this show!

MONTE. (*Already moving eagerly toward bench.*) Oh, all right, if you insist—!

VIOLET. Say, *about* the songs in this show, I was looking at the *lyrics* the other day—

PHYLLIS. (*Rapturously.*) And aren't they simply magnificent?! Monte is *so* talented!

VIOLET. Well, yes, but—one of the *rhymes* bothers me.

MONTE. (*Between bench and piano, but not yet seated.*) Oh? Which rhyme is that, Violet ?

VIOLET. In that duet between Elizabeth and Mary—

PHYLLIS. "The Throne Is Rightly Mine"? One of my absolute favorites !

VIOLET. Yes, that 's the one.

LOUISE. (*Riffling through script.*) But which rhyme–?

VIOLET. The one about "evil aims." Monte rhymes it with "Thames"! (*She pronounces this, of course, as it looks: Thayms.*) Shouldn't that be [*the proper pronunciation:*] temz?

MONTE. Poetic license, my dear. I mean, I *know* the pronunciation of London's lovely river, but *temz* simply wouldn't fit the *moment* in the lyric-line. I mean, the chorus is singing about Mary's "evil aims," and the very *next* bit is about the area's *geography*, in a sense. How else *could* I have handled it ?

SAUL. How about instead of Mary's evil *aims*, you sang about her "sturdy *stems*"? *That* would rhyme with *temz* ...

MONTE. (*Impatiently.*) It would *hardly* suit the moment!

SMITTY. (*Practically.*) But it'd sure suit *Polly*!

GERRY. Smitty! That's not *like* you!

SAUL. (*Grinning appreciatively.*) I *told* you I was contagious! *Nice* one, Smit!

PHYLLIS. Oh, let's stop all this time-consuming palaver and listen to Monte's lovely score!

BILL. Yes, *please*! There's still time for me to get *some* sleep before morning!

MONTE. Oh, very well, if you all insist. (*Will sit at bench as he continues:*) Now, here is that very number we were just discussing—"The Throne Is Rightly Mine"!

*[SPECIAL NOTE: The placement of the piano is not only
because of the sight-line setup. It is because, in case
you cannot find an AGGIE or MONTE who can play
piano, once that dais is in place you can have a pianist
hidden there, to handle the chores of this show's musical
phases, with AGGIE only pretending to be playing (that
bench should be wide enough for two, for obvious
reasons). Since there is no dais at this moment, the
smattering of the music we'll hear (if your MONTE
cannot play, that is) can be pre-recorded for this spot,
which is brief, and played over those onstage speakers
(see PRODUCTION NOTES) in place.]*

PHYLLIS. But first, let me set the scene: Mary and
Elizabeth are having their vital confrontation, alone
onstage except for the chorus, and—
     BILL. Phyllis, we *know* where it occurs! Let's get *on*
with this, okay?
     VIOLET. Bill! The *baby*, remember? It can *hear* you!
     BILL. So it knows Daddy's not a *wimp*! What's the
problem?
     MONTE. Should I *start*, or—?
     BILL. Of *course* you should! *Play*, dammit, *play*!
     MONTE. *(Interlaces and flexes his fingers at arm's
length; then:)* Here we go ...!

*(He plays first chord, pauses, plays second chord, pauses;
so far, so good; OTHERS listen in rapt attention; and
then he starts playing in a sprightly, upbeat fashion,
and OTHERS [except PHYLLIS] start to have a unified
reaction of puzzlement, until MONTE stops playing
as:)*

SMITTY. (*Almost a shout.*) That's "Oh, Susannah"?!

MONTE. (*Impatiently.*) Well, of *course* it is! *All* the music in this show is by *Stephen Foster!*

GERRY. *Banjo*-music in Merry Old England?!

MONTE. Music is what *kept* Old England merry. And a banjo sounds *very* much like a *lute!*

AGGIE. But *we're* using a *piano!*

MONTE. (*Fussily.*) *Only* because I don't know how to score for *banjo!*

PHYLLIS. (*Helpfully.*) Or for lute!

SAUL. (*Sincerely, heavenward:*) Thank you, God!

GERRY. But—if all the melodies are by *Stephen Foster*—?

AGGIE. (*Completing her thought.*) —isn't that ... *plagiarism?*

PHYLLIS. (*Stiffly.*) We *prefer* to think of it as a *tribute!*

LOUISE. On your way to *jail?*

MONTE. The melodies are *all* in public domain. I checked.

VIOLET. But aren't Stephen Foster's melodies—um— sort of innately *American*—?

PHYLLIS. Ah, but you see, Violet, that *bridges* the *gap* between our two nations, which is one of the *major goals* of that marvelous Bess Boosters Society!

SAUL. Let me get this straight: We'll be singing *your* lyrics, but to the tune of things like "Camptown Races," "Nelly Bly," and "My Old Kentucky Home"?

MONTE. Why—*yes*. Why do you ask?

SAUL. I just had a kind of come-full-*circle* feeling, is all. (*To GERRY,with ill-concealed amusement:*) You were *wrong*, Ger. We *can* do this show in blackface!

(*And as GERRY shuts her eyes and shakes her head in chagrin at the near-accuracy of his contention, and PHYLLIS and MONTE stare in puzzlement, and OTHERS start to laugh helplessly at SAUL's observation—*)

BLACKOUT

End of Scene Two

ACT I

Scene 3

AT RISE: Furniture is in the same position, but LOUISE and AGGIE have gone offstage R during the blackout; MONTE is still at piano, but GERRY, SAUL, SMITTY, BILL are standing facing us, with backs toward piano, like people in a police lineup, almost, each with script in hands before them held like hymnbooks; VIOLET is seated on chair at R, and PHYLLIS stands facing quartet from R, about halfway between them and VIOLET; in the fraction of a second before lights come up, we have heard MUSIC-VAMP INTRO, and the instant lights are up:

QUARTET. (*Sings with uncertainty, scanning lyrics in scripts.*)

"Though Good Queen Bess hungered for
True love, true love,
She'd give up a lung before
She'd share her throne!
Still, Essex had her prone
To melt her heart of stone,
But he keeled over on the throne room floor!
Now she must rule all alone!"

PHYLLIS. (*Applauding briskly.*) Marvelous! Simply marvelous! Don't you agree, Monte?

MONTE. (*Stands, a bit uneasy.*) I think we should run the number again.

GERRY. Monte, we've done it at *least* a dozen times *already*!

MONTE. (*Will come around piano to join group, which has un-lined at song's end.*) But this number is the show's *finale*, Gerry! Of all the songs in the show, *this* one should be utter perfection!

SMITTY. I *still* don't understand why *I* should be singing. I mean, the song's *about* me!

MONTE. It's a small group. We need all the voices we can get.

SMITTY. But *mine's* getting so hoarse I can hardly *talk*! I'm in almost *every* number!

SAUL. She's right, Monte. Do you want an Elizabeth with a *rasp*?

VIOLET. It'll be better when *Polly* sings along. *She's* got a *big* voice, and she never sings *flat*!

SAUL. (*Shrugs.*) *Polly's* got a big *everything*! *She* could only sing *chubby*!

BILL. Aw, don't pick on her when she's not *here*, Saul!

PHYLLIS. And why *isn't* she? I thought she *promised* Geraldine that she would *surely*—

GERRY. She'll *be* here! She and Henry were just going out of their house when I called. I'm a little worried about her, to tell the truth. Smitty's cold is affecting her voice, but Polly's is starting to affect her *ears!* I had to *shout* to make her understand who was calling!

MONTE. Oh, dear. Is *Henry* any better?

BILL. Probably not. Whatever Polly gets, *he* gets.

VIOLET. That's what comes of being married so long. It's really kind of charming.

SAUL. So how come he didn't get her *appetite*?

SMITTY. Maybe he did, but by the time *she's* through eating, there's nothing *left* for him.

PHYLLIS. You two should be ashamed. Polly's not really *that* overweight!

SAUL. Listen, the last train trip they took, she told Henry the porter was trying to *avoid* her, when all the guy *actually* said was he planned to give her a *wide berth*!

GERRY. You're making that up!

SAUL. Oh ... well, maybe a little. Relax, first thing when she shows up, I'll blow her a kiss!

MONTE. Do you *mean* that?

SAUL. Well, *sure*. Can you imagine trying to blow her a *hug*?!

GERRY. *Saul!*

LOUISE. (*Off R.*) *Ow!* Aggie, be more careful with that *hammer!*

AGGIE. (*Off R.*) Sorry, Lou.

MONTE. How *are* they coming with that *throne-*contraption? (*Starts R.*)

SMITTY. Almost done, I think. Maybe we should give them a hand. (*Starts R.*)

PHYLLIS. (*Moving after her.*) Oh, and by the way, Marla, there's something I wish to discuss with you about your *makeup* as Queen Elizabeth ... (*As TRIO exits R, from L we hear:*)

POLLY. (*Off L.*) Hi! Anybody here--? (*She and HENRY enter L, bundled up in overcoats, both pink-nosed.*)

GERRY. Oh, good, I was beginning to worry. How are you feeling?

HENRY. My ears still feel a bit stuffy, but it'll go away once the weather improves. (*They'll divest themselves of outer-wear, leave things on chairs L, while SAUL and BILL amble over to sit flanking VIOLET, all during:*)

GERRY. (*Still in DC area below piano.*) I certainly *hope* so. Or this throne room will look more like an outpatient clinic! Are you up to rehearsing your major scene, do you think—?

POLLY. Oh, yes, quite definitely! Sick or not, Henry and I have been over it I-don't-know-*how*-many-times!

HENRY. We're even *off book*! (*Outer-wear disposed of, they move toward GERRY, during:*)

GERRY. Well, good for you! I wish certain *other* people had your dedication...! (*Sidles a glance toward SAUL.*)

SAUL. I'm *working* on it! (*Grabs up script, studies it with furious scowl.*)

POLLY. Well, now! Shall we begin?

GERRY. (*Fumbling in own script, as she eases backward DR, leaving them C.*) Just let me find the page

... *ah!* Here it is: Sir Renfrew, from the Scottish court, has arrived to defend Mary at her trial. Ready, guys?

HENRY. I think so. Shall we begin?

GERRY. Whenever you're ready.

POLLY. Okay, then, here goes! (*Turns her back to HENRY, wrings her hands distractedly.*)

HENRY. (*Steps up behind her, taps her on shoulder; as she turns:*) "I came as soon as I could!"

POLLY. "I can't tell you how delighted I am!"

HENRY. "I'm a bit late because my horse threw a shoe and flung me into a ditch!"

POLLY. "You're lucky you weren't killed!"

HENRY. "I hope my tardiness has not made you angry with me?"

POLLY. "With *YOU*? Never!"

HENRY. "Have you slept well?"

POLLY. "On a pile of straw in the dungeon!"

HENRY. "I am shocked! At least I hope you're being well fed!"

SAUL. (*As POLLY almost replies to HENRY.*) Pause for laughter.

GERRY. Saul Watson—!

SAUL. Okay-okay, but I *do* think Phyllis was *pushing* it with that line! No offense, Polly, but, honey, you do *not* look underfed!

POLLY. (*Ruefully.*) Don't I know it! And it'll be even *worse* when I'm in my *costume*! Gerry, do I *have* to wear that *farthingale*?

GERRY. Polly, it was the *style* of the *era*. *All* the women wore them!

VIOLET. Women are crazy! *Why* wear a style that makes your hips *twice as wide*?!

BILL. Yeah. You know what the women in those things always looked like to me back in the old costume-drama movies? Up-ended *dustpans!*

SAUL. (*Laughs.*) It *is* kind of like that, isn't it! From the waist upward they're the *handle,* and—

GERRY. Can we have this discussion *later?* Or has Bill *forgotten* he *works* tomorrow?

BILL. Oops. I almost *did.* If I come in late one *more* morning, there could be a Help Wanted sign on my office door!

HENRY. Then let's go, shall we?

GERRY. Absolutely!

POLLY. Feed me your line again, Henry.

HENRY. "I am shocked! At least I hope you're being well fed!"

POLLY. "Not lavishly, but I'm too proud to ask for more!"

SAUL. (*Slightly-too-loud murmur to his companions:*) If they *have* any more! (*BILL and VIOLET giggle, not hiding it very well.*)

GERRY. (*Turns to look at them.*) Please...?

TRIO. Sorry.

GERRY. Go on, Henry. Just try to ignore those clowns.

HENRY. (*Trying to remember his place.*) Ask-for-more ... ask-for-more ... ah! (*Into character.*) "I admire your stamina. And they have not, I trust, subjected you to torture?"

POLLY. "That, at least, I have been spared!"

HENRY. "Good. Now, alleviating your situation will require superlative intelligence!"

POLLY. "Not to mention a stalwart horse!"

SAUL. A *very*—! (*Sees GERRY's face, shrivels.*) I'm sorry.

GERRY. You *should* be! Go on, Henry.

HENRY. "I *do* have a plan up my sleeve! I only hope they have a *sidesaddle* for your mount!"

BILL. (*A not-unheard whisper, which he tries to muffle, to SAUL and VIOLET.*) Two sidesaddles.

GERRY. I'd better find that *you* three jokers know *your* lines as well as Henry and Polly, or we'll *see* who gets all the laughs around here!

VIOLET. Gerry, I don't *have* any lines!

GERRY. Don't be silly, Violet. After all the *coaching* you've been doing, you probably know *everybody's* lines!

POLLY. Gerry, can we go *on*? Henry and I aren't *quite* over these darned head-colds yet, and we'd like to finish and sit down.

GERRY. Sure, Polly, sure. (*To POLLY, but for TRIO's ears.*) And there had better be *no more* interruptions! (*TRIO shrivels mousily in unison.*) Take it right after Henry's sidesaddle line.

POLLY. Um ... okay, got it: "I'd be happy to *straddle* it to get away!"

HENRY. Uh ... uh ... oh, damn! What's my line, anyhow?

GERRY. (*Feeding him from her script.*) "The hardest part will—"

HENRY. (*Interrupts.*) Got it! "The hardest part will be getting across the moat!"

POLLY. "I can be quite athletic if I have to!" (*Stops, looks at TRIO; they all widen their eyes in feigned surprise that she'd even think they'd make a crack, and:*)

SAUL. We didn't say a word!

POLLY. You were *thinking* about it!

GERRY. Polly, we *can't* try to enforce *mind*-control among the imbeciles!

POLLY. More's the pity. Go on, Henry. Sorry to interrupt. "... athletic if I have to!"

HENRY. "But do you think you're *up* to such an effort?"

POLLY. "Bah, *nothing* is impossible to a *queen*!"

HENRY. Gerry, this is always a tough transition for me. *What's* the line—?

GERRY. (*Hinting rather than feeding.*) You're still admiring the queen's stamina about being athletic and such.

HENRY. *Ah!* ... "I'm not certain *I* could endure such a strain!"

POLLY. (*Gently complimentary.*) "Sir Renfrew, you have *always,* among the men of my court, stood out from the rest!"

HENRY. "Why, Majesty, I didn't think you'd noticed!"

POLLY. "Now-now, no false modesty! Be of good cheer!"

HENRY. "Ah, but I find it difficult—"

GERRY. Oh, damn!

HENRY. What'd I do?

GERRY. It's not you, it's our playwright! I thought Phyllis had *changed* your line!

POLLY. We *tried,* Gerry, honestly we did. It was tough enough getting her to dump all those *scops* and *baldrics*!

HENRY. But she insisted that, in its proper context, my line would *not* elicit a laugh.

GERRY. (*Shrugs.*) Okay, I give up! Say it, then.

HENRY. "Ah, but I find it difficult to be gay." (*Stops as, abruptly, SAUL guffaws.*) *Now* what?!

SAUL. Sorry. And I really mean that, Henry. But I was following along in the script, and just realized how bad *Polly's* line is, on the heels of *that* one!

GERRY. (*Angrily.*) Saul, if you *continue* to disrupt rehearsals this way—!

POLLY. Wait, Gerry. Saul's absolutely right, I'm afraid. We couldn't get Phyllis to change *my* line, either!

GERRY. (*Blankly.*) What *is* your line—? (*Looks into script, reads for half a second; then guffaws.*)

SAUL. See what I mean, Ger?

GERRY. Wish I didn't! Ah well, ah well, ah well! Let's hope the *pathos* of the scene gets us past this part before the audience has a *chance* to find extra meanings!

HENRY. Amen to that! ... Where shall we—?

GERRY. Back to *your* line, *then* Polly's—and try not to *dwell* on them, if you know what I mean!

POLLY. Do we ever! Hit it, Henry.

HENRY. "Ah, but I find it difficult to be gay."

POLLY. "All the more reason to *try* it, then!"

(TRIO convulses, hands over mouths, but keeps in control.)

HENRY. "At least you have not yet tasted *death*!"

GERRY. (*Applauds, as does the TRIO.*) Beautiful! Beautiful! You guys have *really* been working your *butts* off!

POLLY. Ha! Don't I *wish*! (*Smacks her palms against her ample hips on the line and sighs, while OTHERS laugh good-naturedly.*)

SAUL. (*Amiably.*) Don't feel too bad, Polly. You could get skinny as a snake, and in that farthingale, who'd even *know* it?!

POLLY. *That's* a fact! Say, Gerry, where *is* my costume, anyhow?

GERRY. Still being worked on. It should be ready in a few more days.

BILL. (*By now he and VIOLET and SAUL are standing and stretching a bit.*) I thought we were *renting* the costumes?

POLLY. They're renting the *other* costumes, Bill. But with *my* girth, they have to make one from scratch! If you don't know what I mean, just ask *Saul*!

SAUL. Aw, it's no fun teasing you if you're going to be so good-natured about it.

VIOLET. But think of all the *fines* you'll save!

SAUL. We're not *really* fining me every time I crack wise ... (*Less certainly, to GERRY.*) Are we—?

GERRY. You gotta admit, we could make a *fortune* ...

BILL. Speaking of which—has that *ten thousand* shown up yet?

GERRY. Two days ago. Arrived, signed for, and deposited safely in the bank.

SAUL. How come *I* didn't know about it?

POLLY. Maybe Gerry wrote it in your *script*!

SAUL. (*Winces.*) Ouch!

VIOLET. *Nice* one, Polly!

LOUISE (*Off R.*) Gangway, everybody!

AGGIE. (*Off R.*) This thing weighs a ton!

MONTE. (*Off R.*) At *least*!

(TRIO enters R, staggering beneath the weight of a huge marble-painted throne-dais [this is tall enough so that its upper platform will fit precisely atop the spinet, with at least a two-foot vertical "rim" at upstage edge of this platform which will serve both to keep the throne (when they install it) from slipping off backwards, and to further mask any view of the pianist behind it, and with a series of enough stairs on its downstage side so that The Queen can ascend/descend with ease]; SAUL and BILL will hasten to help them move it, during:)

BILL. What is this monster *made* of, anyhow?!

SAUL. *My* guess is solid *brick! Umfff!* *(QUINTET will get this leviathan settled in its proper place, during:)* Wait, make that solid *lead*!

LOUISE. Hard to believe it's only painted plywood!

AGGIE. But don't forget it's braced with all those *two-by-fours*!

MONTE. Did you have to use so *many*?

POLLY. *(As she and HENRY back out of struggling QUINTET's way.)* It's *got* to support the queen's *throne*, Monte.

SAUL. *(A grunt in mid-effort.)* Good thing *you* don't get to sit on it! *(It's in place; QUINTET backs off a bit to view it, with random sighs and grunts and pants, flexing numb fingers, etc., during:)*

HENRY. How magnificent!

GERRY. It looks like real *marble*, too!

BILL. It *weighs* like real marble! *(Flexing.)* Are my *arms* any longer? They sure *feel* like it!

LOUISE. Look on the bright side, Bill—*now* you'll be able to embrace *Violet*!

SAUL. Too bad *Henry* didn't help out!

POLLY. (*Irked, not amused:*) Oh, ha ha!

MONTE. Oh, dear, I've just realized—it's blocking the soundboard of the piano! (*Starts scurrying U to keyboard.*)

AGGIE. Monte, it *has* to! The piano's the main *support* under the *platform*!

MONTE. But will we be able to hear the *music*—?! (*Quickly bangs out random notes/chords for a moment; then:*) What do you *think* ...?

GERRY. I may be crazy, but—I think it sounds even *better!*

POLLY. Perhaps the dais is acting like an *extension* of the soundboard!

SAUL. Hey, I'll bet Polly's *right!*

VIOLET. But can it still vibrate once the *throne's* on top of it?

BILL. Not to mention *Smitty!*

AGGIE. I sure *hope* so!

LOUISE. Otherwise we may have to drill *holes* all over the thing to let the *sound* out!

MONTE. (*Moving from U of piano to rejoin group, during:*) But how could we possibly *justify* a throne-room dais full of *holes?*

SAUL. You could always say it's *Swiss* marble ... (*Then ALL are distracted by:*)

SMITTY. (*Enters from R, followed by PHYLLIS.*) No, Phyllis, it's out of the question!

PHYLLIS. But Marla, if you are to play Elizabeth looking absolutely *authentic*—?

SMITTY. (*Stops, faces her, arms akimbo.*) Authentic be damned, Phyllis Montague! I am *not* going to shave off my *eyebrows!*

PHYLLIS. But she didn't *have* eyebrows!

SMITTY. Phyllis, she was the wealthiest woman in the world. She could afford *falsies*!

GERRY. Look, could you fight about makeup *later*?

BILL. Yeah, we've got to rehearse these *lines*!

MONTE. What about rehearsing the *songs*?

LOUISE. Not to mention building the *set*!

AGGIE. And *painting* it!

VIOLET. And *I've* still got to design the *program!*

SAUL. So what's *stopping* you?

POLLY. Phyllis hasn't been able to think of a *title* yet, remember?

VIOLET. And I can't send it to the printer with no *name* on it!

HENRY. We can *hardly* call it "Guess What?!"

BILL. If Phyllis keeps *stalling*, we may *have* to!

PHYLLIS. Oh, but there *is* a title for the show, finally!

VIOLET. You could've *told* me!

PHYLLIS. But it only *came* to me last night! As you all know, I've been pondering and thinking and considering for *ever* so long, but I've at last come up with the absolutely most *darling* name for the show—

GERRY. So *tell* us the name!

PHYLLIS. Well, you see, since the main *thrust* of the plot is that Elizabeth, while extremely *flirtatious* by nature, is basically *afraid* of making a romantic commitment—

SMITTY We *know* all that, Phyllis!

VIOLET. What are you calling the show?!

PHYLLIS. (*Takes a breath, then announces proudly, grandly:*) "CHICKEN COQUETTE"!

(OTHERS stare at her in various degrees of aghastness, and remain thus, frozen in place with jaws agape, except for SAUL, who—after a moment of standing as frozen as the rest—suddenly relaxes and turns to GERRY.)

SAUL. *(Almost conversationally blithe.)* Say, here's a novel idea ...

GERRY. *(Unfreezes only slightly, to ask:)* What?

SAUL. Let's do this show *without* a program! *(And as OTHERS all turn to stare at him—)*

BLACKOUT

End of Scene 3

ACT I

Scene 4

AT RISE: Only people onstage are MONTE, GERRY and SMITTY. GERRY is in the process of moving one of the chairs from RC area toward the dais, and she will install this temporary "throne" atop the dais over dialogue. MONTE stands facing SMITTY just D of dais, his hands paternally atop her shoulders.

MONTE. Now, remember, Smitty, although this is the song just *before* the show's finale, it is really the emotional *climax* of the story, so you'll have to *sell* it, pull out all the stops, give it everything you've got!

SMITTY. (*With a definite frogginess in her throat.*) I'll do my best, Monte.

GERRY. (*En route up dais stairs with chair.*) Do you think she should even *try* singing, with that throat of hers?

(*SAUL wanders in from R, eating a sandwich, will take a seat on one of the chairs in the R area, listening to the goings-on.*)

MONTE. Oh, it's a nuisance, I *know*, but she'll be fine if she simply sings *above* it!

SAUL. Vocal coaches always *say* that when a singer's getting hoarse. What exactly does it *mean*?

MONTE. I haven't the *faintest* idea. But, Smitty—will you at least *try* it?

SMITTY. (*Shrugs.*) I'm game if *you* are. (*Ascends partway toward "throne," pauses.*) Where's my prop?

AGGIE. (*Off R.*) Coming right up, Your Majesty! (*Emerges carrying small flowerpot into which is stuck a red pinwheel.*)

MONTE. You call *that* a *gillyflower*?

LOUISE. (*Off R.*) You may as well, we still haven't *found* one!

GERRY. If we could only find a *picture* of one, we could get some crepe paper and *fake* it!

MONTE I suppose you *could* change it, if worse came to worse. I mean, I never mention it by name in my *lyrics*.

AGGIE. (*Has handed pot up to SMITTY, now seated on "throne," and is headed R.*) I sure wish *Phyllis* had your resiliency! (*Pauses for:*) Do you know she found a *picture* of the Windsor Castle throne room, and expects us to *duplicate* it?!

LOUISE (*Off R.*) At the rate *we're* progressing, she'll be lucky to get any walls at *all*! ... Hey, Aggie, what'd you do with my tape-measure?!

AGGIE. I'm coming, I'm coming! (*Exits R.*)

GERRY. (*Now in DR area, facing dais, with script in hand.*) Okay. Places! Let's get this thing rolling!

SMITTY. (*On "throne," holding pot.*) I *am* in place!

GERRY. But Monte isn't!

MONTE. Me? ... *Oh*, you mean at the *piano*! (*Starts heading toward keyboard-side.*) I'm not *used* to actually *playing* at a rehearsal. I keep expecting *Aggie* to do it.

AGGIE. (*Off R.*) I *will*, as soon as we finish building this damned palace!

MONTE. (*Now at piano, out of view.*) Ready when you are, Gerry.

GERRY. On your marks, get set, go!

(MUSIC INTROS, and:)

SMITTY. (*Sings.*)
 "As I dream of dear Lord Essex
 And the love I held so dear,
 It is soothing when I gaze upon
 This blooming souvenir!"

(MUSIC continues for about four beats, then stops.)

GERRY. Why did you stop?

MONTE. (*Coming into view.*) Nobody was singing.

GERRY. Not you. Smitty.

SMITTY. That's where the *chorus* is supposed to come in. I don't sing again till later.

GERRY. (*Looks at script.*) Oh, damn, you're right! (*Yells off R.*) Louise? Where's our *chorus*?!

LOUISE. (*Emerges R, hammer in hand.*) Helping Polly try on her *costume*! She can't do it alone, I guess.

MONTE. But how can we rehearse this *number*?

SAUL. Are you sure it *needs* a chorus? I mean, frankly, *Oh, Susannah!* isn't exactly what I call a tear-jerker, Monte.

MONTE. What do you suggest? I've *already* used up *Beautiful Dreamer* and *Jeannie with the Light Brown Hair*!

GERRY. Not to mention *My Old Kentucky Home* and *Old Black Joe*! I don't think Foster *wrote* any other *wistful* tunes!

SAUL. Maybe if Monte could play it a bit *slower*, or–?

MONTE. But the Bess Boosters have already *approved* this tempo! I can't change it *now*!

BILL. (*Appears in UL area.*) Ready or not, folks, here she comes! (*Steps aside, gestures UL, and then POLLY enters in costume, flanked by HENRY and VIOLET; her royal gown is plaid, and wide as a truck.*)

POLLY. (*Stops, as do HENRY and VIOLET, makes two-handed sweeping gesture at garb.*) Well? What do I look like?

SAUL. Mary, Queen of *Stouts*!

POLLY. (*Who agrees with him.*) Don't rub it in!

GERRY. Isn't that—I don't know quite how to put this—a little *too* plaid?

VIOLET. Maybe it won't stick out so much once everyone *else* is in costume ...

SAUL. If *Polly's* onstage in *that*, you won't be able to *see* anyone else!

LOUISE. Hey, how wide *is* that thing?

SMITTY. (*Who has stood up to look toward POLLY.*) From *here*, I'd estimate Polly could come on carrying a pair of *picnic* baskets—*no hands*!

POLLY. I may just *do* that! They say *stuff* a cold, and mine's worse than ever!

GERRY. Polly, if you *keep* stuffing yourself, it'll take *all* of us to get you into costume!

VIOLET. I took that under consideration when I *made* it, Ger. It's all *Velcro* up the back, to leave room for *expansion*, just in case!

MONTE. Well, as long as you're all *here*, why don't we rehearse the *chorus* part of Smitty's song?

POLLY. (*Turns UL, starts out.*) Let me get out of *this* thing first! I can't *possibly* sing in a tight bodice! (*Exits.*)

MONTE. But how will you sing in the *show*?!

HENRY. She can't *hear* you, Monte. The cold's blocking her ears.

GERRY. Oh, great! I'm glad *you* can still hear, anyhow!

HENRY. As long as I can see your *lips*, I'm just fine! (*Turns and exits UL.*)

MONTE. You mean *you're* going deaf, *too*?! (*But there is, of course, no response; MONTE turns to face GERRY.*) How are either of them going to hear the *music* cues?!

SAUL. We could *always* hide a pair of prompters under Polly's *farthingale*...?

SMITTY. Can I come *down*? These lights are like a *sauna* up here!

GERRY. *Stay* there. It may help your *cold*!

MONTE. This is becoming disastrous! I've got to tell Aunt Phyllis! Where *is* she, anyhow?

AGGIE. (*Off R.*) Out searching for gillyflowers!

GERRY. In an early spring *blizzard*?!

LOUISE. Gerry, she's *not* out romping through the *meadows. Just* the florist's shops. (*Will exit R.*)

MONTE. Good old Phyllis! If I know her, she *won't* come back until she *finds* some!

AGGIE. (*Off R.*) If she isn't any luckier than *I* was, we may never see her *again!*

SAUL. See, Ger? There's a bright side to everything! (*And as OTHERS all glare at him—*)

BLACKOUT

End of Scene 4

ACT I

Scene 5

AT RISE: Only four people onstage: VIOLET is sitting on chair in L area, knitting happily; GERRY is in DR area with script open; BILL, with that pinwheel-pot thing in hand, is in UR area; SMITTY is still seated on "throne," but now holds a fan, which she is using almost without pause, occasionally back-handing sweat from her brow.

GERRY. Okay. Places. Ready, set, go!

BILL. (*Comes down before dais, makes deep genuflection toward SMITTY, on:*) "Gracious Majesty—"

(HAMMERING off R.)

GERRY. Louise! Can you hold *off* for a minute?

LOUISE. *(Off R.)* You want walls, or don't you?!

BILL. *(Who's come to his feet again.)* Can't she come in and do that when we're *not* rehearsing?

LOUISE. *(Off R.)* What do you think, I *live* in this place? *I* have a life, *too,* Billy-boy, *and* a job to get to in the mornings!

BILL. *(Sincerely.)* Sorry, Lou. I'd just like, *once,* to get *through* this scene!

LOUISE. *(Off R.)* I'll get myself a cup of coffee. Then it's hammer-time again!

GERRY. Thanks, Louise! Go ahead, Bill!

BILL. From my *entrance*—?

GERRY. *No!* Let's go right from your line!

BILL. *(Genuflects again.)* "Gracious Majesty—"

PHYLLIS. *(Pops in L, ecstatic, waving a small glossy envelope.)* I found a packet of gillyflower seeds!

BILL. *(Coming to his feet.)* So *plant* them, already!

AGGIE. *(Emerges R, paintbrush in hand.)* How long till germination, Phyllis?

PHYLLIS. *(Still L, reads back of package.)* It says ... um ... first sprouts appear within ten days!

BILL. Look, ladies—

AGGIE. But how long after *that* till we get a *flower*?

PHYLLIS. *(Reads again; then:)* Five to six weeks, if there isn't any frost.

GERRY. Phyllis, we *open* in *three* weeks!

PHYLLIS. Oh, dear. Maybe if we *force*-fed it with *hormones* or something—?

BILL. Can you please discuss this somewhere *else*?!

PHYLLIS. (*Now crosses past him toward AGGIE.*) There is *no* need to raise your *voice*, William!

BILL. (*Nearly at lungtop.*) *That's what you think!*

VIOLET. (*Looks up for first time, chides gently.*) Bill. The baby. It *moves* when you yell.

BILL. Then it 's got better manners than some *playwrights* I know!

PHYLLIS. Well, *really!* (*Exits R with AGGIE, on:*) There must be *some* way to speed these seeds up !

AGGIE. (*En route off R.*) If there *isn't*, Lord Essex may be giving Elizabeth a pretty red *pinwheel*!

GERRY. Come on, Bill, start the scene! Now's your chance!

SMITTY. Yes, *please*, before I *melt* up here! I don't know *how* I'll stand it in *costume*

BILL. I'd be happy to start the scene, Smitty, *if you'll just shut up*!

VIOLET. Bill—

BILL. I know, I know! (*Sings toward VIOLET, very fast and annoyed:*) *Rockabye baby in the treetop*—!

GERRY. Bill, the scene—?

BILL. *OKAY!* (*Drops on one knee.*) "Gracious Majesty—"

(*HAMMERING off R.*)

GERRY. *Louise*, what are you *doing*?!

BILL. (*Still on one knee, through gritted teeth:*) "Gracious Majesty—"

PHYLLIS. (*Pops onstage R, waving packet.*) William, might we borrow that *pot*—?

BILL. (*Comes to his feet, starts left-right-left-right tantrum-stamping of his feet, waving his arms in the air, and screaming at lungtop:*) *Aaaaaaaaaaaaaaaa!* (*And as a wide-eyed VIOLET twists slightly U, leaning forward to shield "baby" from this display with both arms—*)

BLACKOUT

End of Scene 5

ACT I

Scene 6

AT RISE: Stage, looking as we last saw it, is empty. Then GERRY enters L, holding a raincoat almost at arm's length by the fingertips of one hand, shaking it slightly. She steps over to drape it across the back of a chair in L area, and as she does so, her face registers what she's just realized as she looks at stage; she looks dismayed.

GERRY. *Aggie*—?! (*Drops coat over chair, hurries R, stops DC as AGGIE enters R.*) Where's the *set*?! Tomorrow's dress rehearsal! How can we rehearse without a set?!

AGGIE. It's ready, it's ready, Gerry. Calm down!

GERRY. But why isn't it up? People will be here any minute! You and Louise promised—!

AGGIE. I know we did, hut we didn't reckon on this crummy *weather!* A snowy February, a sleety March, and now a drizzly April!

GERRY. What's the weather got to do with—?

AGGIE. The *paint's* not dry! Everything's painted—even Smitty's *throne*—but we can't have people *using* the things in those rented *costumes!*

GERRY. Oh ... damn it all! How can we *open* in two nights if the cast doesn't have a chance to work on the *set?!*

LOUISE. (*Enters R.*) It's not as bad as you think, Ger. I mean, for instance, there aren't any *doors* to open and close, just *archways* for entrances and exits. If they know their blocking, it should be a *breeze.*

AGGIE. Meanwhile, we've got a space heater backstage, hurrying the paint along. We'll be able to set things up later tonight, I'm sure.

GERRY. I wish *I* shared your confidence! Smitty's going to be *furious* if she has to work on that metal folding-chair another night, and I don't blame her!

SAUL. (*Enters L, stops.*) Am I early? Where's the set?

AGGIE. Drying.

SAUL. Damn. Smitty's going to flip out if she has to—

LOUISE. We've already been over that. Her throne's still kind of *tacky*, is all.

SAUL. How do you *mean t*hat?

LOUISE. Both ways. The paint's not dry, and it looks pretty awful, besides.

GERRY. Even with the gold paint?

AGGIE. Even. We *tried* to make it look like *real* gold, but it still looks like wood with a bad gold paint job.

LOUISE. But the *seat's* nicely padded. *That* should help Smitty's morale.

SAUL. I hope so. She tells me her morale has *bruises* from that *other* chair!

GERRY. Say, where *is* she?

SAUL. Don't look at *me*. I haven't driven her in *weeks*.

AGGIE. Then how's she *getting* here?

SAUL. *Monte's* been bringing her. Do you people mean you don't *know* about those two?

LOUISE. (*Eager for juicy gossip.*) *No!* When did all *this* start happening?

SAUL. (*Moving to join group in area between dais and R wings.*) When she caught her cold. Monte's been giving her *private* coaching lessons.

AGGIE. Wow! Does *Phyllis* know? (*This is said just as that very lady enters L.*)

PHYLLIS. Do I know *what*, Agatha?

GERRY. It's nothing, Phyllis. Trust me. Just—an idle rumor.

PHYLLIS. (*En route toward group, stops dead.*) The *show*?! Someone's been taken *ill*?! The *costumes* didn't fit?!... *Oh!* Where's the *set*?!

SAUL. Relax, Phyl. It has *nothing* to do with the show.

AGGIE. And the set's perfectly fine—

LOUISE.—as soon as the paint dries.

PHYLLIS. (*Relieved, moves again toward group.*) Well, *that's* a mercy! But then, what were you talking about when I arrived? What *is* this idle rumor? (*At this moment, MONTE and SMITTY, in cuddly arm-in-arm, enter L, stop.*)

SMITTY. *Hi*, everybody! *We're* going *steady!*

PHYLLIS. (*Staggered.*) *WHAT*?!

MONTE. (*In seventh heaven.*) I asked her on the way over here, and she said yes!

PHYLLIS. But—*Monte*—Marla is—is a mere *girl!*

MONTE. What *should* I go steady with, a mere *pony*?

PHYLLIS. But Monte!

SAUL. Relax, Phyllis, Monte's got a *girl*, not *Bubonic Plague*! (*SMITTY sneezes violently; he adds:*) That comes later.

LOUISE. Monte, if you can unhitch from your gal a minute, *I* have to talk to you about that cockamamie *computer* you wangled for us!

MONTE. (*Unhitches, starts across toward her, leaving raincoat with SMITTY.*) You're not having troubles *again*, are you, Lou? What's the problem *now*?

LOUISE. I put *all* the sound-effects in, and now I can't get them *out!*

MONTE. Maybe you just need a new battery in the beeper.

LOUISE. *What* beeper?

MONTE. That little flat gadget, like a remote control for a TV. I mean, if you're going to be on and off stage playing that *messenger* part, you obviously have to be able to control the computer without being at the keyboard!

LOUISE. But if I'm onstage without my *script* in front of me, I don't know all the *cues!*

MONTE. (*Takes her by one elbow, guides her off R, on:*) Oh, come on, I'll show you. It's easy as pie!

SMITTY. (*Has put MONTE's raincoat over chair, followed by her own, now turns and starts toward group, but stops dead as she looks up on dais.*) Where's my *throne*?! Aggie—?

SAUL. It's *okay*, Smitty, trust me! All ready for you as soon as the paint's dry!

SMITTY. If *that's* the problem, why not *put* it on the dais? It's so warm up there I nearly got *heatstroke* last night! Gerry, do I *have* to sit so near the *lights*?

GERRY. I'm afraid *so*, honey. If we didn't use that *dais*, how could we hide the *piano*?

SAUL. Put *Polly* in front of it!

AGGIE. You know, with that *farthingale* of hers, it might *work!*

SMITTY. But then where *would* I sit?

SAUL. Polly could carry you on her shoulders!

GERRY. *Saul!*

SAUL. You have a *better* suggestion?

(BILL and VIOLET enter R, reacting to tableau as they doff raincoats.)

BILL. Hey, where's the set?!

PHYLLIS. Maybe we should put a *sign* on the stage door!

SAUL. Why, Phyllis, that was very nearly a *wisecrack!* I'm proud of you!

AGGIE. It's what she gets for hanging around with *theatre* people! *(Turns and exits R, on:)* What's keeping you two? Smitty's getting jealous!

SMITTY. Of *Louise*—?!

SAUL. I hope she didn't hear you. You could get roasted alive on the dais if she gets her hands on the light-control rheostat!

VIOLET. (*As she and BILL now cross toward group.*) You still didn't answer Bill's question ... where's our *scenery*?

SMITTY. (*Sits glumly on dais steps.*) The whole stupid *set* is still soaking *wet*!

BILL. Hey, that's pretty good! Monte been teaching you lyric-writing on the side?

SAUL. It's hard to be in a musical and *not* start thinking in rhyme. Just listen to the beauty *I* thought up the other day: (*Sings, to tune of CAMPTOWN RACES:*) What was Ben-Hur's *given* name...? (*Points to SMITTY, who stares, then gets it, and:*)

SMITTY. (*Finishes musical phrase cheerily:*) Judah! Judah!

PHYLLIS. Hush! Monte will *hear* you! It's not *nice* to make fun of his lyrics!

(*POLLY and HENRY enter quietly, L, start doffing outerwear, their noses even pinker than before.*)

BILL. But he *wasn't*. Just making up lyrics of his *own*. Pretty *good* lyrics, too!

VIOLET. Oh, *I've* got one! (*Sings, same melody:*) Name a wise man from the East! (*Points to PHYLLIS.*)

PHYLLIS. Oh, but really, I'm not very good at—oh! (*Gets it, sings prettily:*) Buddha! Buddha! (*OTHERS except GERRY whoop and applaud, as PHYLLIS preens shyly.*)

POLLY. (*She and HENRY are moving toward group now, looking uncertain.*) What's *that* you're singing? We're not fiddling with the *lyrics*, are we?

HENRY. I don't think I could *take* any changes at *this* point ...

GERRY. And there aren't any! It's just clown-time at the O. K. Corral! Have you people forgotten we have a *rehearsal* tonight? And we *open* in two night!

SMITTY. (*Stands.*) Sorry, Ger. But it *was* fun—

SAUL. I didn't know our Miss Montague had it *in* her!

PHYLLIS. Now, Saul, don't be so formal. It's just plain "Phyllis," after all the time we've *worked* together!

SAUL Why, *thank* you, Plain Phyllis!

GERRY Do ... you ... people ... mind—?!

BILL. Right! Let's serious up! What's our first move, Madame Director?

GERRY. Get into your costumes, and we take the show from the *top*! Now, *move*!

MONTE. (*Entering from R, with AGGIE and LOUISE.*) Wait a minute—I think we have a problem!

GERRY. So what *else* is new?!

AGGIE. We can't figure out who's going to operate the *computer* when we run the show!

PHYLLIS. Can't you just draw straws, or—?

LOUISE. It's not the *choice*, Phyllis, it's the logistics!

SAUL. What do you mean?

AGGIE. Somebody, one *person*, has to be in charge of that *beeper* at all times. I mean, the computer's running the *lights*, it's running the *sound*, and everything's been programmed in *sequence* on it.

GERRY. But I thought *Louise* was going to handle that? I mean, she's not playing that messenger *all* the time, and even if she *is*, if she keeps the beeper *with* her—?

LOUISE. But I have to be able to *see* what's happening, and I can do *that* only when I'm *on!*

GERRY. Can't you kind of hover in the wings, and *peek* onstage?

LOUISE. With all those *farthingales* trying to get by me? It'd be like getting caught in a *car*-wash!

GERRY. Then ... *Aggie*—?

AGGIE. While playing the piano *and* prompting? Impossible!

SMITTY. *I* could do it, but I'm involved in so many *songs*, I could *forget* ...

PHYLLIS. Well, then, why don't *I* handle it? Since I'm not *in* the show—

SAUL. But you *are*, Phyllis! You don't *mean* to be, but you get so happily *absorbed* watching your show unfold that you forget there's *tech* involved!

AGGIE. Remember that *last* show of yours we did?

GERRY. All you had to do was bring that *pendant* backstage at the proper moment, and when the time came, you were still seated *out front*!

PHYLLIS. Oh, dear. I *do* tend to get involved in the *story*, don't I! Well, how about *Monte?*

MONTE. I *could* do it, if I weren't playing the Spanish Ambassador! (*To GERRY.*) Are you *sure* you couldn't get any more *men* to be in this show?

GERRY. *Men? Men* trying out for a show? Monte, *you* don't know much about *community theatre!*

POLLY. You're all fussing over *nothing. I'll* do it! Where's that beeper?

MONTE. Here it is, Pol. But your role is so *prominent*—where will you *hide* the thing?

POLLY. (*Shrugs.*) In that stupid *farthingale*, of course! I could hide an *army* in there!

LOUISE. But do you know all the *cues?*

HENRY. Polly and I know this script *backwards!*

SAUL. That's what we're *afraid* of!

POLLY. Don't be silly, Saul. Louise, is this thing hooked up?

LOUISE. All batteried up and ready to roll, Polly.

POLLY. Then, let's go: *Try* me on those effects!

(NOTE: Bracketed items in following are the sounds we'll hear.)

GERRY. You're on!

POLLY. Okay! Now, it's right after my big scene with Henry, right?

LOUISE. Right...? So what happens?

POLLY. It's time for *Elizabeth's* entrance, so I tap the beeper, and—

[FANFARE]

SAUL. So far, so good.

POLLY. Elizabeth has just learned that Essex has escaped from the dungeon, *and* that the Spanish *Armada* is on the way! She's just announced this when—

[FANFARE #2]

—Louise runs in to tell her that Lord Essex is on his way to the palace, and as the commoners outside the window see him passing—

["HOORAY!" etc.]

So Elizabeth orders the drawbridge lowered at once, and—

*[SOUND OF SLIDE-WHISTLE (DESCENDING.) AND
    LOUD THUD]*

MONTE. *Hold* it!

POLLY. That was *right*, wasn't it?

MONTE. The *cue* was fine, but—*Louise*, where did you
get that *sound*?!

LOUISE. I couldn't find rattling-chains. I figured the
whistle would have to do.

PHYLLIS. But it sounds so—so *silly*!

LOUISE. Just tell the Bess Boosters that a well-*oiled*
drawbridge *sounds* like that. Ten-to-one they've never heard
a falling drawbridge, *anyhow*!

PHYLLIS. Wellll ...

BILL. Come on, Phyllis, be a sport! We can't risk
fiddling with the *computer*-memory! You *know* how
temperamental those things are.

PHYLLIS. Oh, very well, let it go. If everything *else*
turns out all right, probably no one will notice. Go ahead,
Polly, what's next? *You* remember my show better than *I*
do!

POLLY. Okay. Essex comes into the throne room,
genuflects, and says—

BILL. (*Down on one knee before SMITTY.*) "Gracious
Majesty, I have returned!" (*Stands, says to GERRY:*) I need
all the rehearsing of that line I can *get*!

SMITTY. And *I* say, "Be still, my heart!", and—

HENRY. Hit it, Polly!

[PA-TUMP, PA-TUMP, PA-TUMP]

PHYLLIS. Beautiful! Absolutely beautiful!

BILL. "I bring you a gift, Gracious Majesty, as penance for my abrupt departure. A delicate Swiss concoction to mark the merry hours, thus:"

[COO-KOO, COO-KOO, etc.]

SMITTY. "How charming! Let the cannons speak to the heavens to show my acceptance!"

[KA-BOOOOOM!]

AGGIE. Polly, *you* are a *marvel!*

VIOLET. *Then* what happens?

SMITTY. I place it on the little stand beside the throne, where I keep *all* his gifts—

LOUISE. *Yipe!* Aggie, we forget to get that *stand!*

SMITTY. *What?* I can't hold all those things in my *lap!*

GERRY. Wait! I've got a little taboret at home that'll be just the thing! It's not painted *gold,* but it's darned pretty...

SMITTY. Wellll ....

SAUL. It'll be fine, Smitty, fine. Go ahead, Polly.

POLLY. Uh ... wait a minute ... it'll come to me ... uh...

SMITTY. Oh, it's *my* fault, I didn't *cue* her. Polly, here's where I place the clock beside the gillyflower and the little music-box from Essex—

PHYLLIS. The *gillyflower!* Aggie, has it *sprouted* yet—?

LOUISE. Doesn't have to! We made one from some wire and crepe paper, from the illustration on that seed-packet!

PHYLLIS. How *resourceful*!

AGGIE. And *this* one won't *wilt* under the *lights*!

SMITTY. Which is more than *I* can say! Oh, anyhow, Polly, I pick *up* the music-box, and—

POLLY. Oh, yes, now I remember !

[TINKLE-TINKLE OF MUSIC-BOX]

GERRY. That's when *I* look out the window and announce a courier approaching !

[GALLOP-GALLOP OF HOOVES, RUNNING FEET]

SAUL. Who's the courier?

MONTE. It's not *really* a courier, Saul, it's *me*, the Spanish Ambassador! I stride up before the throne, announce that the Armada is in sight, and that your cowardly people are fleeing in terror!

[Voices doing "RUN!... HURRY!... GET A MOVE ON!" etc.]

BILL. That's *my* cue to gesture dramatically and say that *heaven* will defend our shores! I shout this to the commoners outside the window, and—

[Cheers of "WONDERFUL!... MARVELOUS! ... YIPPEE!" etc.]

SMITTY. But I'm dubious, and I say, "How so, Lord Essex?"

BILL. And I say, "The *sea* shall destroy them!" and we hear—

[THUNDERCLAPS, VERY LOUD]

GERRY. *Wow!* Polly, you didn't miss a *one!*

SAUL Maybe Saint Genesius won't have to work *quite* so hard this show!

MONTE Who ?

SMITTY. The patron saint of actors. We pray to him every opening!

MONTE. Is there a patron saint for *musicals*?

PHYLLIS. Let me see ... Saint Cecilia?

AGGIE. Well, *she's* more for instrumentalists. *I* get to pray to *her!*

GERRY. *Enough!* We can work out heavenly assistance *later!* Right now, we have to *work!*

VIOLET. Just one thing before you start—Monte, you never told me how many *tickets* to set aside for those Bess Boosters opening night. I saved about a dozen, just in case, but I'd like to sell the ones we *don't* have to reserve .

MONTE. The Bess Boosters?! Why, *they're* scattered all over the *country!* They weren't coming here *in person*, Violet.

LOUISE. Then *how* are they supposed to see the *show*?

GERRY. That ten thousand bucks goes *back* to them if we don't *do* the show. I thought seeing it was our only *proof!*

MONTE. But they *will* see it. I've arranged for a special *WATS* line to be hooked up to the *computer*, with an electronic videocamera at the back of the auditorium. They can see the show *live*, from the comfort of their living rooms!

GERRY. Why, Monte, how ingenious!

VIOLET. And it means that I can sell *all* the tickets for opening night!

SAUL. Which we won't *have* if we don't start *rehearsing* soon!

PHYLLIS. Yes, and no performance, no ten thousand dollars! They'll want the money *back*!

GERRY. We'll make it, Phyllis. We always do, somehow. And we've *got* two nights to give it all we've got!

MONTE. *Two* nights?

GERRY. Tonight, and tomorrow night.

MONTE. You—you don't *open* tomorrow night? I was *certain* it was tomorrow night!

SMITTY. (*With foreboding.*) Monte—what have you done...?!

MONTE. (*Shattered.*) Set up the telecasting of the show for *tomorrow*!

PHYLLIS. Well, *un*set it, quick!

MONTE. I *can't!* There's a *waiting*-list for those WATS hookups. It's tomorrow night or not at all!

GERRY. You mean the Bess Boosters are going to see our *dress rehearsal*?

SAUL. Gerry, maybe we'd better say an *additional* prayer to Saint *Elmo*!

BILL. The patron saint of *sailors?* Why?

SAUL. Because I've got this *sinking* feeling!

POLLY. What'll we *do*?! We haven't even practiced on the *set*!

HENRY. Or worked with all the *props!*

SMITTY. Or practiced *moving* in those *costumes!*

VIOLET. And we're opening a day *early!*

GERRY. With *ten thousand bucks* riding on our success!

PHYLLIS. Geraldine, I'm sure it will be *fine,* so long as you don't have to *halt* things for *corrections!* I mean, the Bess Boosters *are* expecting a *performance* for their endowment ...

SAUL. No *stopping*? In one of *our* dress rehearsals?! How can we possibly *do* it?

LOUISE. The same way we *always* do it!

AGGIE. And how, exactly, is *that,* Louise—?

LOUISE. *(Folds her hands before her breast, looks heavenward, and:)* Saint Ge-*neee*-si-us...?!

OTHERS. *(Take same stance instantly, and shriek heavenward in unison:) HELLLLLP!*

THE CURTAIN FALLS

End of Act I

ACT II

Scene 1

There is no curtain-rise for this first scene; until PHYLLIS steps out on the apron, we see nobody yet, but we hear everybody quite clearly [This can be done simply by having your players speak their lines directly through the curtain toward the audience, or by utilizing those onstage speakers (see PRODUCTION NOTES), whichever is more easily audible.]; so, then, HOUSE LIGHTS GO DOWN, and we hear:

GERRY. Polly, are you *sure* you and Henry are *feeling* all right?

POLLY. *What* did you say, dear?

GERRY. HOW DO YOU FEEL?!

POLLY. Oh, fine, dear, just fine. And the makeup hides our red noses wonderfully!

GERRY. It's not your *noses* I'm *worried* about! How is your *hearing*?

HENRY. There's no problem, Gerry. Polly and I have rehearsed so thoroughly that we can say our lines *without* hearing each other!

POLLY. After all, in our *big* scene, we just *alternate* lines. When Henry stops, I start, and vice-versa!

BILL. I can't find that gillyflower!

AGGIE. Who took my sheet-music?

LOUISE. Polly, you forgot the *beeper!*

85

POLLY. *What* did you say, dear?

MONTE. Has anybody seen my false moustache?

SMITTY. My *crown* won't stay on this stupid *wig!*

PHYLLIS. Here, let *me* help, dear!

VIOLET. No, let *me* do that, Phyllis, *you* have to get out there and make your *speech!*

PHYLLIS. Oh, dear, where did I put my notes?

SAUL. *Notes*?! How long *is* it?!

MONTE. Aunt Phyllis, that WATS hookup-time is *limited!*

PHYLLIS. But I *really* should say *something* before we begin...?

GERRY. Just wish the audience welcome, say hi to the Bess Boosters, and get *off!*

MONTE. We *have* an audience?

AGGIE. We always have at dress rehearsals. Mostly friends and relatives. Gives us some kind of audience-response to *play* against!

MONTE. Oh, that's wonderful! The Bess Boosters will be *impressed* when they hear the *audience* applauding!

LOUISE. "Applauding"? You don't know my relatives!

PHYLLIS. Don't tease, Louise! Truly, when they hear Monte's lovely lyrics, just *imagine* the applause!

SAUL. We may *have* to!

GERRY. SAUL.

SAUL. *Only* kidding!

HENRY. *What* did he say?

GERRY. Henry, can you hear *anything*?

HENRY. I assure you, Gerry, our hearing will be *quite* adequate to the task! Isn't that *right*, Polly?

POLLY. *What*?

SMITTY. (*Just slightly raspy.*) Has anybody got a cough drop?

MONTE. We've got to get *going*! The WATS-line hookup started fifteen seconds ago!

SAUL. *Phyllis*, get *out* there!

PHYLLIS. But my *notes*—!

MONTE. *Wing* it!

PHYLLIS. Oh ... very well, I'll do my best!

GERRY. Positions, everybody! Overture goes the moment Phyllis comes back!

SMITTY. We forgot to pray to Genesius!

SAUL. And Saint *Elmo*!

OTHERS. CUT THAT OUT!

GERRY. Come on, everyone: Saint Genesius—

OTHERS. *Pray* for us!

PHYLLIS. Well—here goes *nothing*!

SAUL. That's what we're *afraid* of!

GERRY. SAUL!

SAUL. Sorry. (*Then PHYLLIS steps out on stage before the curtain, and:*)

PHYLLIS. Good evening, ladies and gentlemen, and *welcome* to the World Premiere of a simply *marvelous* musical saga of the life and times of Queen Elizabeth the First of Merry Old England. Of course, she didn't *call* herself "the first," because she had no way of *knowing* there would someday be an Elizabeth the *Second*—

GERRY. (*From behind curtain, a loud whisper.*) Get *on* with it, Phyllis!

PHYLLIS. (*Slightly rattled, does her best.*) But that is neither here nor there, as they say! So, if you will all just sit back and relax—*oh*! I forgot to welcome the Bess Boosters! (*Waves toward "camera" at rear of auditorium.*)

Hi there, Bess Boosters! (*Then to live audience.*) You see, we have this electronic *hookup* to this world-famous group—

MONTE. (*Behind curtain.*) But not for very *long*, Aunt Phyllis!

PHYLLIS. *That* was my nephew Monte! A *most* talented young man, who has written all the simply *stirring* lyrics to the show you are about to see—

SAUL. (*Behind curtain.*) —*sometime* this *year*!

PHYLLIS. I—I guess I've taken *enough* of your time! Very well, then! It is time for the World Premiere of CHICKEN COQUETTE! (*With a merry wave.*) Let the revels begin! (*As PHYLLIS exits from stage, we hear, all lines from behind curtain:*)

SMITTY. (*Mournfully.*) "Revels"? Ha!

AGGIE. At least she didn't say, "Gentlemen, start your engines!"

GERRY. *Aggie*, will you start the *stupid overture*—?!

SAUL. That'd be *my* description of it!

OTHERS. *Saulllll*—! (*And as OVERTURE begins—*)

End of Scene 1

ACT II

Scene 2

SCENE: *When we see the set, it will really look pretty darned good. There are walls, finally, with two entries: an archway UL and a matching archway UR; an open-*

casement window in L wall shows a glimpse of sky or Olde Englishe Tudor-style houses, shops, etc. That gilded-wood throne is finally atop the dais, with arms, back and seat padded in purple velvet; GERRY's borrowed taboret sits R of throne where SMITTY can reach it; a tiny music-box sits on the taboret.

AT RISE (which comes immediately at end of OVERTURE): We find CHORUS onstage (in this show, CHORUS is anybody onstage at any given time who is not doing a solo, duet, or other featured spot); SAUL, in Major-Domo outfit and tall staff, stands at attention just R of R archway; LOUISE, in messenger-garb, is just entering through archway; and GERRY, in lady-in-waiting outfit, stands just DL of dais.

LOUISE. I bring news to the royal lady-in-waiting! Where is she?

SAUL. Waiting over there!

LOUISE. Hail, lady-in-waiting! (*Approaches her.*)

GERRY. (*Out front.*) Gadzooks, it is the royal messenger. (*To LOUISE as she arrives.*) What tidings bring you ?

LOUISE. It grieves me to announce—the king is dead!

SAUL. Alas! Say 'tis not so! (*Will move D to join them.*)

LOUISE. Alas, '*tis*! Ah, but wallow not in mawkish grief, for Elizabeth his daughter has just been crowned queen!

GERRY. Her mother Anne Boleyn would have been *so* proud!

SAUL. Then this is no time for gloom! 'Tis time for festivity!

LOUISE/GERRY. Verily, yea !

[NOTE: This is a song-cue, but for the benefit of those just reading this script who have not yet ordered the musical score, the original name of the Stephen Foster tune will be indicated in parentheses at the start of each song, so you can sort of "sing along" in your head.]
(MUSIC INTROS, and:)

TRIO. (*Sings, to tune of "NELLY BLY"*:)
    Defunct defen-
    Der of the faith
    Has drawn his final breath!
    So goodbye, Hen-
    Ry the Eighth!
    Hail, Elizabeth!

(SMITTY enters via L archway, will move down toward them, fan in hand.)

    Each voice shall coo!
    Each lute shall strum
    Elizabeth's success!

SMITTY. (*NOTE: She should not sing raspily, nor speak that way during show, but her voice should weaken gradually toward end of her time onstage.*)
    My full name's too
    Cumbersome!
    Call me "Good Queen Bess"!

(Will start ascending dais, but not sit on throne, during:)

TRIO.
> Her rule sure
> Brings future
> Freedom from all dreads!

SMITTY.
> All who disown
> My royal throne
> Soon shall lose their heads!

CHORUS.
> Did you hear that?!
> We wonder what
> Her reign may have in store!

SMITTY.
> In nothing flat,
> My foes will rot,
> 'Cause when I reign, I pour!

TRIO.
> What if your reign
> Begins to pain
> The court aristocrats?

SMITTY.
> If they talk back,
> They're gonna lack
> A place to wear their hats!

TRIO.
> We'd better
> Not get her
> Mad one teensy speck!

ALL.

    To keep life fine,

    Just toe the line,

    Or get it in the neck!

    By heck!

SMITTY. Now then, what royal duties lie upon my agenda today?

GERRY. The bestowing of knighthoods, your majesty, but *first* an audience with the ambassador from Spain!

SMITTY. How very tiresome! Ah, well, send him hither! (*SAUL starts move back UR, but stops at her blurted mutter:*) Oh, *damn* it—! (*The reason for this mutter is that she has attempted to sit upon the throne, and the arms of the chair have come up beneath her pair of side-jutting extensions of the farthingale, rising up partway so that she seems to be in the jaws of a fabric fish; she stands, tries to sit again, can't do it without same result, so gives it up and resourcefully turns slightly sideways, sitting on right haunch on throne, with right leg dangling over right chair-arm, on:*) There!

SAUL. (*Uncertainly.*) Should I—um—*summon* the ambassador still—or *what*?

GERRY. (*Calming his confusion, flicking backs of fingertips at him.*) Yes-yes, at *once*, of *course*!

SAUL. (*His line was a reply to SMITTY's last scripted line, but now goes directly to GERRY:*) Your will is my command, gracious majesty! (*Realizes this has gone awry after one more step UR, turns for:*) Or whoever you are. (*Takes former beside-arch stance, raps twice with staff on floor.*) The Spanish Ambassador!

MONTE. (*Steps onstage through other archway, realizes his error aloud:*) Oops! (*Dashes from view behind*

UC wall, re-emerges through R archway, back in character, strutting proudly down toward dais.) Gracious Majesty! I come upon a matter *most* urgent—*(Has now rounded lower R corner of dais, sees SMITTY's sitting-stance.)* Uh ... uh ... uh ...? *(Looks to LOUISE helplessly.)*

LOUISE. The queen *always* sits like that, Monte—I mean, *Diego!* *(When he still just stares at her, numbly, she expounds wearily:)* Saddle-sores! *(Exits UR.)*

MONTE. *(Trying to get back on track.)* Dreadfully sorry, your majesty!

SMITTY. *You're* sorry!

GERRY. *(Hinting.)* But what *is* this *matter most urgent...?*

MONTE. Matter most—? *Ah,* yes! *(Back in character.)* We understand your majesty has *seized* Mary of Scotland and brought her *here!* Be warned that she is a *particular* friend of King Philip of Spain, and should she come to harm, you must beware the consequences!

SMITTY. What nonsense you talk, Don Diego! Why, Mary is my cherished *cousin!* Why should I *not* seek out her companionship for mere happy hobnobbing?

MONTE. You brought her here in *chains!* And you threatened her with *execution!*

SMITTY. A silly misunderstanding! I chanced to admire her accouterments, and whilst in the presence of my royal executioner, didst vouchsafe the opinion that I'd like to have her *kilt!* The man misunderstood. I scarce was able to forestall him in time ere he carried out what he deemed my royal command!

MONTE. You *still* haven't explained the *chains,* majesty!

SMITTY. Nor do I *intend* to do so! I tire of this persiflage! Begone hence! I have myriad matters of more import to pursue!

MONTE. (*Bows, backs in DL direction, on:*) Very well, majesty. But mark my words, I shall *return* if all be not well with Philip's friend! (*Starts toward L exit, realizes error, tiptoes, fast, U of dais, and makes his exit properly through R exit.*)

SMITTY. (*Fanning herself [she will do this every so often in short spurts, doing it at very frequent intervals as show progresses in length].*) La, what an annoyance! Now I must *forbear* doing away with Mary until I know better what international *perils* such an act might provoke! (*Shrugs petulantly; then:*) And now, where are the candidates for knighthood?

SAUL. *Oops!* (*Galvanized, he exits R up behind UC wall.*)

GERRY. (*Covering.*) Coming shortly, I ween, majesty. Mayhap he forgot to *change* for the ceremony!

SMITTY. (*Ad-libbing hopelessly.*) Mayhap you're right. Mayhap. How—uh—*long* do you think it'll take him?

GERRY. Ohhh ... not *very*. I ween.

SAUL. (*Only his arm appears, tapping twice with staff U of archway, on:*) Gracious majesty, the first of the candidates for knighthood—the renowned playwright William Shakespeare! (*Staff is withdrawn and we hear it CLATTER ON FLOOR, then SAUL comes briskly around edge of archway and moves toward throne, his high-forehead wig in place, a quill pen in his hand; he proceeds to dais, bows, and:*) Your majesty! I congratulate you on your coronation! And am deeply pleased that you have chosen to mark the happy occasion by bestowing *knighthood* upon me!

SMITTY. A gracious gift from the crown most richly deserved by you, the perpetrator of such pretty little plays! So if you will *kneel—(Looks about her, panics, murmurs:)* Now—um—*what* did I do with that *sword* ... the one I *always* use for stuff like this?

GERRY. *(As if there were anyone else to do so:)* I'll get it! *(Gallops UR, getting sword from PHYLLIS's outthrust hand just before entering archway; takes it and gallops back to R side of dais.) Here* it is! *(Raises it, one hand on the handle, one on the tip, to SMITTY.)*

SMITTY. Thanks a lot! *(Back into character, stands, moves to front lip of dais.)* Approach and kneel, William! *(He does so, kneeling midway up steps; she raises sword.)* Do you accept this singular boon?

SAUL. Oh, *yes*, majesty! Matter of fact, out of gratitude I have written a new *play*, completed just last evening, to *honor* your coronation day!

SMITTY. How thoughtful! And what is the *title* of this play in honor of this great day?

SAUL. *(Proudly.)* "MUCH ADO ABOUT NOTHING"!

SMITTY. *(Lifts sword just before it can touch his shoulder, tilts it back so dull edge of the blade rests upon her shoulder; tilts her head toward GERRY, and says, definitely disgusted:) Next!*

SAUL. *(Rises.)* Aw, shucks ! *(Head hanging, shoulders slumped, he shuffles off R, but while still in view, bolts R to get behind UC wall, and that staff appears again in R archway, as he continues in Major-Domo voice:)* Announcing the second candidate for knighthood: Walter Raleigh! *(We hear staff CLATTER ON FLOOR again, and then SAUL bounds into view in R archway, plumed cap on his head, long cloak swirling from his shoulders; unhappily, he still wears high-forehead wig as he comes down toward dais, but he halts his move as he hears:)*

LOUISE. (*Leaning into view from R side of archway.*) *Pssssst!* (*When he looks her way, she points at her own forehead, whispers loudly:*) The wig...!

SAUL. (*Realizes, whips off cap, whips off wig, replaces cap, hands wig to GERRY, continues toward dais.*) Gracious majesty! How honored I am to be so honored at your coronation! It is an honor! (*Elsewhere, GERRY—with an inane grin—has wig behind her out of sight, and "surreptitiously" backs to R archway, where LOUISE pops out long enough to take wig from her, then pops back; GERRY now eases herself downstage toward throne again; all this happens during:*)

SMITTY. And one you richly deserve, for your many fascinating explorations of the new world to the west, *and,* if I may say so, for your conspicuous *gallantry!* (*SAUL is D of dais, on its R side, now, still facing out front; now he takes a step to foot of dais, turning his back upon us as he does so, and dropping upon one knee before SMITTY, and we see that his cloak has—from lower right corner diagonally up to his left shoulder—a series of muddy female footprints on it.*)

SAUL. It was nothing, your majesty.

SMITTY. You are too modest, Walter. Approach and be knighted! (*He goes up a step or two, kneels, and she taps him lightly upon his shoulder with the sword, on:*) I dub thee—*Sir* Walter Raleigh! (*She steps back, he ascends one stair higher, still on his knees, on:*)

SAUL. And *this*, majesty, is for *you*! (*Hands her slip of folded paper.*)

SMITTY. A *thank-you* note?

SAUL. A *payment*-voucher for my *dry-cleaner*! It's *tough* getting stains out of *silk*!

SMITTY. Ha! As I *live*, you do but *jest*, Sir Walter! (*Tears voucher firmly in two, adds in more ominous tones:*) ... as *you* live! Right?

SAUL. (*Gets to his feet, backs down to foot of dais.*) But of course! A jest! A feeble jest! I *knew* you would be amused by it! I hope.

SMITTY. Lady-in-waiting—? What *further* matters of state impend?

GERRY. *None*, your majesty, for the moment!

SAUL. (*In area L of dais.*) What? No royal denunciation of the duplicity of Robert Devereux Lord Essex, who has dared to deign to share your reign?

PHYLLIS. (*Off.*) I *love* that line !

VIOLET/LOUISE. (*Off.*) Ssh!

(*NOTE: For the most part, unless otherwise indicated, players onstage do not react much to offstage speeches; they're having enough problems.*)

SMITTY. It is hard to rule alone! Tempted I am, if truth be told, *to* share my kingdom!

GERRY. But royal protocol demands that you not *think* of marriage to a commoner! A lord, yes; royal blood, no.

SAUL. And Essex is ambitious! Soon it would be *he* and not *you* who would rule the land!

GERRY. You must, beseems, *forswear* his ardent pursuit of your heart, majesty!

SMITTY. Alas, would that 'twere not so! (*MUSIC INTROS, and she sings to tune of "OLD BLACK JOE" :*)
>Gone are the days kissing 'neath the mistletoe!
>Essex must pay for his plotted overthrow!
>As England's queen, I must keep the *status quo*,
>But, as a woman, *wow*, it's hard to
>Hold … back … woe!

(Song is ended; after a fractional pause, GERRY and SMITTY look toward SAUL, who has just been standing in one spot all along; he reacts to their looks blankly, until:)

GERRY. Gee, I'll bet it 's nearly time for that Major-Domo to *announce* somebody again!

SAUL. *Oops*! (*Runs, exits L, reappears almost immediately through R archway minus plumed hat, with that staff in hand again, but still wearing the Raleigh-cloak; he raps the floor twice with staff from his now-location just R of archway, and:*) Majesty! I beg to announce the arrival of your arch-rival, Mary Queen of Scots, under heavy guard!

(HENRY enters R, his "guardship" signified by a helmet, steps to L side of archway, gestures back toward area U and R of archway, on:)

HENRY. And here comes that doughty and defiant dowager now!

*(POLLY appears in archway, and then The Worst occurs:
In full farthingale, she cannot fit through archway;
OTHERS wait it out, paralyzed with dismay, as
POLLY struggles valiantly to make a frontal entrance,
finally gives it up, and sidles onstage through archway;
puffing a bit, smoothing her farthingale, she moves
down to point just R of dais, and:)*

POLLY. Good morning, "dear" cousin!

SMITTY. Why stand you there? Do you not bow to England's queen?!

POLLY. As yet, to my mind, England *has* no queen. At least, not the *right* one!

SMITTY. Oh, *that* old argument! As a direct descendant of my father, it is *I* who rule! Your claim is worthless! And if you keep *on* about it, I have a headsman just *itching* to silence your nattering once and for all!

POLLY. Do you dare to *threaten* me?

SMITTY. As the absolute monarch of this land—why *not?* I dare *anything*!

POLLY. But that's just the *point,* girlie! *I* don't agree that you *are* a monarch! (*MUSIC INTROS and she sings to tune of "OH, SUSANNAH!":*)

> You're a lovely lady, Lizzie,
> And your palace is divine,
> But I'm really in a tizzy
> 'Cause the throne is rightly mine!

CHORUS. (*GERRY in L-of-dais area, HENRY and SAUL flanking R archway, and a quickly-popping-into-view LOUISE, who will stand between the men.*)

> Mary Stuart!
> Your claim comes much too late!

> For your head will soon be skewered
> On a pike above the gate!

SMITTY.

> Though we share a common ancestor,
> And royal blood is thine,
> I'm not taking any chances, for,
> The throne is rightly mine!

CHORUS.

> Good Queen Bessie!
> Your claim she'll never jump!
> She will find the crown is messy
> When it's perched upon a stump!

POLLY.

> If you dare to lay a hand on me,
> I'll tell the King of Spain!
> His armada will put out to sea
> And come to end your reign!

CHORUS.

> Liz, be wary!
> Forestall her evil aims,
> Or we'll all be drinking sherry
> At the bullfights on the Thames!

MONTE. (*Off.*) Beautiful! Beautiful!

VIOLET. (*Off.*) *Ssh*!

SMITTY.

> I can muster up a navy, too!
> What do you think of that?

POLLY.

> Like a Yorkshire pudding's gravy, you
> Will soon be cold and flat!

ALL.

> Two contenders♭

The throne is up for grabs!
And if neither one surrenders
We may all end up on slabs!
Like rotting crabs...!

(Song's ended; duty done, LOUISE right-faces and exits.)

GERRY. Oh, my beloved queen, what *will* you do? E'en though your claim be just it sure won't keep us from getting blown to *nada* by that armada!

SMITTY. It *is* a point to ponder! Excuse me, whilst I confer with my ministers! *(Descends from dais; OTHERS bow as she turns and exits L.)*

POLLY. I wonder—whilst Elizabeth absents herself—if I might just take a kind of *quickie* perch upon the royal throne? Just to get the *feel* of royal ruling!

GERRY. Nay, 'tis impossible!

SAUL. Yon throne was built for better buttocks than thine own!

HENRY. *(Glancing off R.)* Say, isn't that Lord Essex approaching? And not even under guard!

GERRY. He doth elude them most merrily *all* the time! How *doth* he do it?!

POLLY. They durst not lay hands on one so handsome!

BILL. *(Appears in R archway.)* Announce me at once, Major-Domo!

SAUL. Robert Devereux Lord Essex hath arrived—*hast* arrived—*hath* arrived—he's *here*! *(Shaking his head in confusion over the line, SAUL turns and exits via R archway; GERRY is already headed that way, and:)*

GERRY. 'Tis time for tea! Let us hasten apace to the larder lest all the scones be consumed ere our appearance there!

HENRY. A sound suggestion, indeed! *(Lets her precede him off R, then exits himself.)*

BILL. *(Having clumsily avoided this triple-egress without quite being pushed back offstage, lurches a step onstage, now, and:)* Forsooth, where *is* my beloved? I see her not!

POLLY. You're not missing much! An unlovely conglomeration of pompous pride, bad manners, and store-bought hair!

BILL. Ah, but, Queen M., I *love* Queen E., and do range through many a restless night in romantic reveries of her soft surrender to my manly machinations!

POLLY. Is there *insanity* in your family, Lord Essex? How can you *stand* the woman?

BILL. *(Shrugs.)* Through perils dread, in my lonely bed, I just can't get her outa my head! *(MUSIC INTROS and he sings to tune of "JEANNIE WITH THE LIGHT BROWN HAIR:)*

> I dream of Queen E. with the bright orange
>   wig!
> Though she lacks eyebrows, I don't care a fig!
> Once we are married, and go out anywhere,
> I shall never have to wait while she does her
>   hair!
>
> Such a sweet advantage is hair you simply
>   don!
> Waiting will be scant as she just pops it on!
> And so, no wonder that I feel so sublime!

It's a gas to love a lass who's always on time!

POLLY.

Your brain is teeny and you think like a flake!

There's more than punctuality at stake!

All right, you'll never have to say, "Shake a leg!"

Even so, who wants a bride who's bald as an egg?

BILL.

From her I'll not drift, even though long locks she lacks!

POLLY.

As a bridal gift, you can buy Turtle Wax!

BILL/POLLY.

I/So dream of Queen E. and avoid lover's pangs!

BILL.

What a girl ...!

POLLY. (*Points to her own occiput and winks at audience on:*)

So like a *pearl*...!

BOTH.

... behind bogus bangs!

POLLY. Well, if you'll excuse me, I'm missing my tea! (*Will turn and exit regally UR, an exit messed-up only for a moment as she once again "jams" at archway, forgetting she won't fit; she recovers, gives a pretty little laugh, then sidles off R.*)

SMITTY. (*Steps into view in L archway, sees BILL, stops.*) So *there* you are, you would-be usurper of the throne!

BILL. (*Who was in R-of-dais area, steps D a bit, eyeing her.*) And there *you* are, a mere statue of a woman with a heart of coldest marble!

SMITTY. (*She will move toward him, and he toward her, until they meet D of dais.*) You plot to steal my kingdom!

BILL. You forswear the merriment of marriage!

SMITTY. You are ambitious!

BILL. Your blood is ice water!

SMITTY. You are bold!

BILL. You are cold! (*They are D-of-dais now, about a foot apart.*)

SMITTY. I despise you!

BILL. I despise you *more*!

SMITTY. There is but one word for a man of your singular ilk!

BILL. And that word *is...*?

SMITTY. (*Meltingly.*) Darling!

BILL. (*Rapturously.*) Darling! (*They go into fabulous clinch/kiss, and MUSIC INTROS, and as they break:*)

SMITTY. (*Sings to tune of "BEAUTIFUL DREAMER":*)

> Though you should die for
> Craving my throne,
> I've got an eye for
> You when we're alone!

BILL.

> In my embrace, you
> Knock my goals down!
> I'd rather chase you
> Than plot for your crown!

SMITTY.
>Beautiful schemer!

BILL.
>Hot-blooded queen!

BOTH.
>Is love supreme, or
>Will doom intervene?

SMITTY.
>Life's everything glum!

BILL.
>Love's an abyss!

BOTH.
>Each time we cling, chum,
>My mind goes amiss!
>Crave I the kingdom
>As much as your kiss?!

(They clinch/kiss again, ardently, passionately; while they do:)

VIOLET. (*Off.*) That should have been *me* out there doing that!

PHYLLIS. (*Off.*) In *your* condition? Impossible!

LOUISE. (*Off.*) How *are* you feeling, Violet?

VIOLET. (*Off.*) Kind of tired, and I'm developing the *awfullest* backache!

GERRY. (*Off.*) Oh, dear! *You* don't think that—?

VIOLET. (*Off.*) With the *show* going on? I don't *dare* think that!

SAUL. (*Off.*) Damn. Who's the patron saint of *slow deliveries*?!

LOUISE. (*Off.*) The U.S. Post Office!... Oops! Excuse me, I've got an *entrance!* (*Pops into view in R archway, carrying that crepe-paper-gillyflower in its little pot; she clears her throat delicately, and this is the signal for BILL and SMITTY to break clinch and look guilty.*) Sorry to interrupt—uh—*matters* of *state*—but you asked me, Lord Essex, to bring this to you right after tea-time!

BILL. Ah, yes! Thank you, royal messenger! Bring it hither!

SMITTY. Why, what a lovely little blossom!

BILL. (*Takes it from LOUISE, presents it to SMITTY.*) One perfect flower to another!

SMITTY. It is beautiful, Essex. I shall treasure it long after you are in your grave!

BILL. You *still* intend to have me executed, my darling?

SMITTY. Your ambition leaves me no other option. Now go, go back to the dungeon, and await the headsman's axe on the morrow! Royal messenger, see that he does so!

LOUISE. Well—I'll do my best ... Of course, he's a lot *bigger* than me! (*Takes BILL by elbow, steers him UR.*).

BILL. I shall not fight you. That would take a man of heart—and my heart is no longer my own possession!

SMITTY. Oh, Essex—! Go not thus to thy doom in the dungeon's midnight gloom! (*But he exits without turning back, LOUISE with him; as MUSIC INTROS:*) How cruelly do the demands of office wreak havoc upon my womanly heart! (*Sings to the tune of "MY OLD KENTUCKY HOME":*)

> In the dungeon's night
> Lies his cold and yucky home,
> Till dawn when the sun has a-rizz!

Headsman's axe so bright
Will chop off his plucky dome.
He who plotted for my crown shall lose his!

(GERRY, LOUISE, SAUL [as Major-Domo now without the Raleigh cloak], POLLY, MONTE and HENRY [in cloak/hood with axe as executioner] appear now, three in each archway-area, GERRY, LOUISE, SAUL and MONTE coming onstage a few steps, POLLY and HENRY [in different archways] remaining framed by archway, but still a bit U of OTHERS, for:)

CHORUS.
Weep no more, Good Queen Bess!
SMITTY.
At least, when he falls dead,
He'll have no more need
To employ his brush and comb!
CHORUS.
Once his noodle rolls, don't cry!
Look ahead!

(This last bit should be unfortunately stressed as though it read: "...Don't cry, Look! A head!")

SMITTY. Oh, I cannot bear it! I cannot bear it! *(Sobbing, clutching the gillyflower to her heart, she rushes UR, exits through archway, barely making it past POLLY's farthingale; HENRY, in L archway, exits L to get out of executioner's getup; POLLY manages to sidle onstage through R archway, and ALL onstage move D to congregate at foot of dais; all this during:)*

GERRY. The queen will be *devastated* when she sees the *dinner* menu for tonight!

LOUISE. Why? What are we *having*?

SAUL. Noodle rolls!

MONTE. Were she not my sworn enemy, I would pity the woman!

POLLY. I know *I'd* hate to be in her shoes! Though I'd *love* to be in her *crown!*

LOUISE. The intrigues of the royal court are mind-boggling indeed!

GERRY. It *is* hard to keep abreast of matters!

SAUL. If *you're* having problems, just think of the *audience!*

(MUSIC INTROS.)

CHORUS. (*Facing out front, sing to the tune of "SWANEE RIVER" [the bits in parentheses are mid-melody "fill-ins," backing up the main melody]:*)
> In case you find it hard to take in
> Such tangled plots,
> (Let us give you a summing-up:)
> Queen Bess refuses to be shaken
> By Mary Queen of Scots!
> (But in the meantime,)
> Love for Essex drives her gaga
> As his doom draws near!
> (But that part is still coming up!)
> So, for a wrap-up of this saga,
> Sit back and lend an ear!

HENRY. (*Appears in L archway in "lawyer" outfit: a graduation gown-and-cap.*) Hail! Which one of you is Mary

Queen of Scots? (*But POLLY still stares smilingly out front.*)

GERRY. (*Improvising desperately.*) She'll be right with you! (*Nudges POLLY.*) Oh, will you look who's here!

POLLY. (*Cups hand behind ear.*) What—?

LOUISE. (*Goes face-to-face with POLLY, moving her lips with readable exaggeration, while POLLY squints hard to see what's being said.*) It ... is ... your ... *lawyer* ... from ... *Scotland!*

SAUL. (*Similarly to POLLY over LOUISE's shoulder.*) He's ... here ... to ... help ... you ... beat ... the ... rap!

POLLY. Oh! My lawyer! Yes! Thank you. (*Back into character.*) Now, *leave* me, I pray, that I may contemplate my foreordained doom! (*Faces out front, wringing her hands tragically, as GERRY, SAUL, LOUISE and MONTE scurry UR and exit, and then we hear:*)

GERRY. (*Off.*) I'm terribly worried about Polly! I don't think she can hear *anything!*

BILL. (*Off.*) *I'm* worried about *Violet!* Honey, are you *sure* you shouldn't call the doctor?

VIOLET. (*Off.*) I'm fine, darling, just fine! The strain of worrying about the *show*, that's all.

GERRY. (*Off.*) Then *I* should have a worse backache than *you* do!

LOUISE. (*Off.*) It'll be okay, Ger. Those two know their lines perfectly. All they have to do is *alternate* speeches, whether they can hear each other or not!

HENRY. (*Who has been making his way downstage with solemn dignity during the foregoing speeches, now takes a stance just U and L of POLLY who still faces tragically out front; he clears his throat, then speaks:*) I came as soon as I could! (*When POLLY still stands there, not looking his way:*)

GERRY. (*Off.*) Why doesn't she *answer*?

LOUISE. (*Off.*) Did he remember to tap her on the shoulder? That's her cue to turn and speak!   •

PHYLLIS. (*Off.*) Let me try to sneak a peek ... (*Pokes her head quickly into view from R of R archway, pops back.*) Maybe when she doesn't *turn*, he'll remember!

HENRY. (*With some puzzlement, says his next line.*) I'm a bit late because my horse threw a shoe and flung me into a ditch! (*Now he remembers, and taps her shoulder.*)

POLLY. (*Turns at once, but naturally says her first line:*) I can't tell you how delighted I am!

GERRY. (*Off.*) That's her *first* speech!

HENRY. I hope my tardiness has not made you angry with me?

POLLY. You're lucky you weren't killed!

LOUISE. (*Off.*) But they're alternating *anyhow*! *He* must he as deaf as *she* is!

HENRY. Have you slept well?

POLLY. With *YOU*? Never!

(*There will be audience-laughter here, and the DUO can seem to dimly be aware of it, squinting out into the audience uncertainly, POLLY briefly twisting a forefinger in her ear, then shrugging, and HENRY, with a puzzled knitting of his brow, faces her again, and goes on:*)

HENRY. I am shocked! At least I hope you're being well fed?

POLLY. On a pile of straw in the dungeon!

HENRY. I admire your stamina! And they have not, I trust, subjected you to torture?

POLLY. Not lavishly, but I'm too proud to ask for more!

PHYLLIS. (*Off.*) *Here,* Louise! You're a royal messenger! Get this note to them at once! We've *got* to get them back on the proper track!

HENRY. Good. Now, alleviating your situation will require superlative intelligence!

POLLY. That, at least, I have been spared!

(There will he more audience-laughter here; POLLY and HENRY do similar business to what they did at last laugh-interruption, and while they do:)

LOUISE. (*Off.*) This note's kind of hard to *read*—

GERRY. (*Off.*) Their *light's* better *on*stage!

LOUISE. (*Off.*) Who's the note *for*?

PHYLLIS. (*Off.*) *Polly*! Now, *hurry*!

HENRY. (*He and POLLY once again valiantly striving to go ahead.*) I *do* have a plan up my sleeve—! (*But then he halts, as:*)

LOUISE. (*Practically gallops onstage and down to the twosome, note extended.*) An urgent message for the queen! (*HENRY reacts to her, and—following his puzzled look— POLLY turns to face LOUISE, too, and then:*)

BOTH. (*One hand apiece cupping an ear apiece:*) *Whaaaat*—?

LOUISE. A *message*! For the *queen*!

HENRY. (*Gamely, takes note from her, ad-libs:*) Uh ... thank you.

LOUISE. (*Desperately.*) For the *queen*!

HENRY. (*Oblivious to her words, reading note*) I'm reading, I'm reading!

LOUISE. (*One last try, flailing a finger in POLLY's direction.*) FOR THE *QUEEN*, you lamebrain! (*But HENRY is looking at note, not at her, and:*)

POLLY. (*Thinks she understands that fingerpoint, say grandly:*) You have my royal permission to depart!

LOUISE. (*Smacks palm to her forehead in despair, moves UR and exits on:*) Oh, damn damn *damn* damn damn! (*HENRY continues to squint at note, POLLY waiting patiently, during:*)

MONTE. (*Off.*) What did you *say* in that note, Aunt Phyllis?

PHYLLIS. (*Off, wearily quotes:*) "You're out of synchronization; *drop one line and* go *on!*"

LOUISE. (*Off.*) Except *now*, unfortunately, *Henry's* gonna drop the line!

BILL. (*Off.*) Anyone for brandy?

SMITTY. (*Off.*) How are you fixed for *cyanide*?

HENRY. (*To POLLY.*) Sorry for the delay, my dear. Hard to read this without my *glasses*—(*Catches himself.*)—matter of fact, glasses haven't even been *invented* yet! Makes it even harder!

POLLY. (*Who can't catch a word of this, queries uncertainly:*) What—what was *in* that *very* unexpected message, Sir Renfrew?

HENRY. (*Has tried to understand, but can't.*) Whaaat—?

POLLY. (*As one doing a charade-mime, but with verbal backup:*) WHAT [*Shrugs.*] ... WAS [*Thumbs back over one shoulder.*] ... IN [*Makes thumb-forefinger "circle" with left hand, pokes right index finger into it*] ... THAT NOTE [*Points at note twice, once on each syllable*]?

HENRY. (*Gets it.*) Ah! (*Hands note to her.*)

POLLY. (*Who reads faster than HENRY.*) Ah! (*Stuffs note into bosom of dress, but obviously feels the audience deserves some sort of explanation for it, so ad-libs out front:*) Uh ... Harrod's department store is having a sale on queen-size beds! (*To HENRY.*) You were saying ...?

HENRY. (*Can't hear her, but recognizes a visual cue when he sees one, and, as per the note, skips his next line [that "sidesaddle" bit], but "feeds her" the line that would have led to it, to get things rolling:*) I was saying—I *do* have a plan up my sleeve!

POLLY. (*Thinking she's got it straight at last.*) Not to mention a stalwart horse!

PHYLLIS. (*Off.*) Oh, dear!

HENRY. The hardest part will be getting across the moat!

POLLY. I'd be happy to *straddle* it to get away!

ALL. (*Off. A concerted groan of helpless despair.*) Ohhhh...!

HENRY. But do you think you're *up* to such an effort?

POLLY. I can be athletic if I have to!

HENRY. I'm not certain *I* could endure such a strain!

POLLY. Bah, *nothing* is impossible to a *queen*!

HENRY. Why, majesty, I didn't think you'd noticed!

SAUL. (*Off.*) You gotta admit, it's no sillier than the *right* way around!

POLLY. You have *always*, amongst the men of my court, stood out from the rest!

HENRY. But it's so difficult to be gay, majesty!

POLLY. Now-now, no false modesty! Be of good cheer!

HENRY. At least you have not yet tasted *death*!

POLLY. All the more reason to *try* it, then!

GERRY. (*Off.*) Hey, that's our *cue* to come back *on!*

SAUL. (*Off.*) How can you *tell*?!

LOUISE. (*Off.*) Never *mind* the cue—we've *got* to get out there! Polly's *still* out-of-sync, and she's got the *sound-effects* beeper!

PHYLLIS. (*Off.*) Oh, no ... *no* ... *NO!*

BILL. (*Off.*) Can't we get by *without* the sound-effects?

MONTE. (*Off.*) You'd have to turn off the *computer*— and that would cut the broadcast to the Bess Boosters!

GERRY (*Off.*) And ten thousand bucks go down the drain!

LOUISE. (*Off.*) So let's *go*, already!

(*Onstage, during the foregoing, POLLY and HENRY have been waiting with rising panic, glancing UR, seeing no one, giving one another meaningless smiles, idly punching one fist into the opposing, palm, etc., swinging their arms, tapping one foot, stretching, stuff like that; their relief is quite evident as suddenly OTHERS IN SCENE come running onstage via UR archway: These are GERRY, SAUL and LOUISE, with SMITTY bringing up the rear: She stops, composes herself to look dignified in archway, while SAUL skids into place just R of archway, and raps the floor twice with his staff as GERRY and LOUISE slow to a sedate strolling-pace near DR corner of dais, on:*)

SAUL. Her gracious majesty Elizabeth has returned!

(*POLLY is watching him, and as he pauses, she quickly jabs her right forefinger down into middle of her farthingale on that side, and we immediately hear*)

FANFARE #1; SAUL is shaken, but he doggedly goes on and finishes his speech:)

SAUL. Make way for the queen!

(Same business with POLLY for every misplaced sound-effect henceforth, of course, so we won't enumerate her following moves, to that beeper, here; naturally, we now get FANFARE #2, as SMITTY enters and strides regally down to forefront of dais, where she will ascend to vicinity of the throne, but not sit down, all during:)

GERRY. Her majesty seemeth overwrought!

LOUISE. I do fear she brings dreadful tidings that bode ill for our land!

GERRY. I do dread to hear them!

LOUISE. Heed thee now, our precious queen is about to speak!

SMITTY. *(In place on dais, now will start to speak with an audible croak.)* My subjects, I have just learned that Lord Essex, contrary to his promise, did *not* go to the dungeon, but fled the palace! Worse than that, reports have come to me that a vast armada of Spanish ships is e'en now appearing on the horizon!

["HOORAY!" etc.]

(NOTE: Our players know they are doomed, but will continue with grim determination despite the sound-effects arriving wrongly.)

LOUISE. (*Rushes toward window on:*) Hark! What is that tumult and turmoil outside? (*Looks out through window, turns to announce:*) Majesty! All may not be lost!

SMITTY. *What* say you, royal messenger—?!

LOUISE. (*Facing SMITTY, but pointing out window.*) Delight of delights! It is Lord Essex, e'en now arriving at the palace!

[SOUND OF SLIDE-WHISTLE (DESCENDING) AND LOUD THUD.]

SMITTY. Then lower the drawbridge at once!

[PA-TUMP, PA-TUMP, PA-TUMP!]

POLLY. (*Audible to us, but not supposed to be.*) Henry, this bodice is stifling! Can you loosen it a bit in the back?

HENRY. *Whaaat*—?

LOUISE. (*Returning from window, has heard, quickly moves behind POLLY.*) Here, let *me* do it! (*As she fumbles with it, BILL, small cuckoo-clock in hand, comes rushing in via UR archway toward D end of dais.*)

SAUL. (*Taps staff.*) Announcing Robert Devereux Lord Essex!

BILL. (*Looking up toward SMITTY.*) Gracious Majesty, I have returned! (*And as he genuflects, LOUISE simultaneously undoes POLLY's Velcro, and we hear a loud rrrrrip!, and BILL springs to his feet, horrified, his free hand feeling about at the seat of his tights seeking the gap.*)

LOUISE. (*Sensing his confusion.*) It's *Velcro*, Lord Essex!

BILL. (*Still at sea.*) What *is*? (*Then sees her just re-doing POLLY's bodice-back, and sighs:*) Wow, is *that* a relief!

GERRY. (*Desperately.*) You were *saying*—?

BILL. (*Lurches back into character.*) Gracious Majesty, I have returned!

SMITTY. (*Croaks raspingly:*) Be still, my heart!

[COO-KOO, COO-KOO, etc.]

BILL. I bring you a gift, Gracious Majesty, as penance for my abrupt departure. A delicate Swiss concoction to mark the merry hours, *thus—(And as he extends clock up toward her:)*

[KA-BOOOOOM!]

SMITTY. (*Staggers, as do OTHERS except POLLY and HENRY, but goes on gamely:*) How charming! Let the cannons speak to the heavens to show my acceptance!

[TINKLE-TINKLE OF MUSIC-BOX.]

SMITTY. I shall place it here, beside my throne, with all thine other tender tokens of your love! Such as this most precious music-box— (*Picks it up in her hand.*)— which plays the melody of the first time we danced in delicate delight! (*Opens music-box and:*)

[GALLOP-GALLOP OF HOOVES, RUNNING FEET.]

GERRY. (*It's all pretty hopeless, but what the heck; rushes to window.*) Lo, a figure on horseback approaches our palace gates! Mayhap 'tis a courier with news of even *more* ill aspect!

SMITTY. Why say you that? The news perchance might *not* be dire ...!

GERRY. Then, majesty, why approacheth the man so *swiftly*? (*Points out window.*) *Harken* to the sound!

[*"RUN!... HURRY!... GET A MOVE ON!" etc.*]

SMITTY. (*Straining to talk over incipient laryngitis.*) Those are the sounds of *haste*, I must agree! But who *is* this courier?

MONTE. (*Appears in L archway and strides down before the throne, on:*) No courier, Elizabeth, but *I*, the Spanish ambassador, with one final offer for you: Surrender your throne to Mary Queen of Scots, or bear the brunt of my countrymen's unconquerable armada!

SMITTY. Never! My armies fear no power on earth! My people will fight to save me!

MONTE. (*Sneers.*) *Your* people? Lily-livered cowards, one and all! Just *listen* to their response upon sighting the armada's approach—!

[*Cheers of "WONDERFUL!... MARVELOUS!... YIPPEE!" etc.*]

SMITTY. Nevertheless, I disdain and despise your ultimatum! I may perish, mayhap, but I shall *still* die a royal *queen*!

BILL. (*Rushes to window, shouts out:*) People of England! We need not fear the might of Spain! We need fear *nothing* under the blessed blue sky, because surely *heaven* will defend the right! So *demonstrate* your contempt for that puny power approaching our shores, set down your muskets, stand proudly tall as Englishmen, and do not even *attempt* to fire *one* single cannon-shot in the enemy's direction! Are you *with* me, men of England?

[THUNDERCLAPS, VERY LOUD.]

SMITTY. (*Uncertainly, very raspy.*) But Essex, how shall the overcoming of our foe come about?

BILL. (*Facing her, points dramatically back out window.*) The *sea* shall destroy them! (*POLLY dutifully pushes at beeper, but of course there is silence, since the thunderclap was the final sound-effect; after about two seconds of this silence, with OTHERS onstage cocking an ear window-ward in vain, Bill lamely improvises:*) Of course, it will do so *quietly*. In—in honor of your coronation day!

SMITTY. Oh, Essex, the kingdom is saved! Come to my waiting arms and *take* me—I am *yours*!

BILL. (*Takes one step her way, stops, clutches his heart.*) Oh! The strain has been too much! My heart ... I think ... I feel ... (*Falls "dead" in area near window.*)

MONTE. (*Kneels, takes Bill's pulse.*) Alas! He is no more! He was my sworn enemy—but ever a valiant foe!

GERRY. Oh, Majesty, how sits this sad circumstance with you now? (*MUSIC INTROS, and:*)

SMITTY. (*Stands tall, smiling tragically, opens her lips and barely squeaks first word of song:*) As ... (*MUSIC

CONTINUES FOR A FEW MORE NOTES, BUT STOPS, as SMITTY's lips work frantically, but nothing comes out of her mouth.)

SAUL. *(Improvising [in fact, all speeches until next Music-Intro will be improvised by everybody onstage.])* The queen is *speechless* with grief!

GERRY. *(To SMITTY.)* Why don't you go get a drink of *water*, majesty?

LOUISE. Or *something!*

MONTE. *Anything!* *(SMITTY nods helplessly, hurries down dais steps, and rushes out UR.)*

VIOLET. *(Off.)* Smitty, can you talk at *all*?

PHYLLIS. *(Off.)* Her *lips* are working, but nothing's coming out!

GERRY. *(She and OTHERS have obviously heard this, and she responds at once.)* Say, I'd better go give her a hand! I mean, a queen shouldn't pour her *own* water! *(She has said this en route to UR, and is now off, and we hear her:)* Can't she make *any* kind of sound? Her big *song* number's coming up!

VIOLET. *(Off.)* Wait! I've got an idea! Gerry—Phyllis—Smitty—you'll have to give me a hand!

(OTHERS onstage now valiantly do their best to make talk, even a very confused POLLY and HENRY, who don't quite know what's happening, but can sense from the OTHERS' panic that it's time for lots of ad-libbing.)

POLLY. *So!* You've come all the way from Scotland to defend me! Nice trip?

HENRY. (*Trying valiantly to read her lips.*) Strip? *Who's* gonna strip?

LOUISE. (*To SAUL, who has left his "post" now, and come downstage.*) How *lonely* it must be for Mary, so far away from the other Stuarts in a foreign land! I'll bet she misses her family!

SAUL. I didn't know she *had* a family.

LOUISE. Just her son, James.

SAUL. (*With some of his usual sneaky glee.*) Well, well! I guess a woman of her age *could* be the mother of *James Stuart!*

POLLY. (*Senses they're talking about her, cups hand behind ear, and:*) *What* did you say, dear?

MONTE. (*To LOUISE.*) The hearing's always first to go!

GERRY. (*Appears in UR archway.*) The queen returns!

OTHERS EXCEPT BILL. (*LOUISE, SAUL and MONTE in wonderment, POLLY and HENRY in deafness:*) What?!

GERRY. And she—she did *more* than just get a drink of water—she decided to—um—*surprise* the royal court by the introduction of a *fancy* new *fashion: One* farthingale, worn *facing* the *front!* And—um—*here* she comes *now...!* (*And VIOLET—looking very much like SMITTY, wearing the other's gown, minus the farthingale, and the wig and crown in place on her head—appears in archway as GERRY steps aside and gestures toward her.*)

SAUL. Hey, that's—

LOUISE. (*Claps a hand over his mouth, adds deftly:*) — *lovely!* Absolutely *lovely!*

VIOLET. (*Will move to foot of dais, ascend steps, and sit upon the throne [she will fit, of course, without the farthingale] over her line and next few speeches; being very pregnant, her ascent will be a waddle.*) Thank you, my subjects, thank you all!

MONTE. (*Still kneeling beside BILL, whose head rises to sight on the speaker, since he recognizes the voice as VIOLET's, firmly presses BILL's head back down to the floor, during:*) Poor man! With his failing strength, he *still* longs for your love, majesty!

VIOLET. But he *is* dead, right?

AGGIE. (*Behind dais.*) Gerry, what's going on—?! (*This is a whisper, but of course we can all hear it.*)

GERRY. (*Waves a shushing hand toward AGGIE while speaking to SMITTY.*) And when he *did* perish, majesty, just before you went out for a *drink*—of *water*—*what* were you saying...?

VIOLET. (*By now on throne.*) *I* wasn't. *You* were.

GERRY. (*Realizes.*) Oh. Right. (*In character.*) Oh, majesty, how sits—

VIOLET. (*Looking with dismay toward taboret.*) Hold it! Where's that gillyflower?

LOUISE. It isn't *there*?

MONTE. (*Desperately.*) Does it *matter*?

VIOLET. (*Uncertainly.*) Well, I *was* going to—um—sing about it. If you know what I mean.

LOUISE. Shall I go *fetch* it, gracious majesty?

MONTE. (*Slides up sleeve and looks at wristwatch; even if it hasn't been invented yet, he forgot to remove it when getting into costume.*) There isn't *time*!

SAUL. So sing *about* it, but sing *without* it!

VIOLET. (*Dismally, but gamely.*) Mayhap I *must*! Pray go *on*, lady-in-waiting!

GERRY. Uh ... Oh, yeah! Oh, majesty, how sits this sad circumstance with you now? (*MUSIC INTROS, and:*)

VIOLET. (*Sings to tune of "OH SUSANNAH!" again, with new set of lyrics:*)

> As I dream of dear Lord Essex
> And the love I held so dear,
> It is soothing when I gaze upon
> This blooming souvenir!

(*Unfortunately, her hands go to her distended belly at this moment.*)

CHORUS. (*OTHERS onstage minus BILL, of course.*)

> Oh, Queen Bessie,
> He's gone, but still you've got
> A reminder of his love within
> That pretty little pot!

VIOLET. (*Stands, hands to belly, apparently feeling some discomfort.*)

> To remain aloof in majesty
> I've reasons by the score,
> But my royal robe of office
> Seems not fitting anymore!

CHORUS.

> Good Queen Bessie,
> Too long for him you've pined!
> You must concentrate instead upon
> The sprout he left behind!

(*By now, CHORUS realizes the unfortunate other message of their words, but they're stuck with the lyric, so plunge bravely onward, trying not to think about what they're singing, and trying not to break up as VIOLET winces in pain and continues:)*

VIOLET.
    Though a queen,
    I'm still a woman!
    It's a fact I cannot hide!
    So the world shall shortly know about
    This stirring deep inside!
CHORUS.
    Dear Queen Bessie,
    The world will shortly know
    That beneath the robe of royalty
    Love must be free to grow!
VIOLET. (*Fearing the worst, starts wobbling down the steps of the dais.*)
    As it grows and grows,
    I'm certain
    To conceal it would be wrong!
    And the truth about his gift I can't
    Contain for very long!

(GERRY, LOUISE and even POLLY realize what's happening, and hasten to assist VIOLET down steps and up toward R archway, during:)

CHORUS.
    Please, Queen Bessie,
    When push has come to shove,
    Let the kingdom be informed about
    The flower of your love!

VIOLET. (*Manages to turn head downstage just short of exit, for:*)
> To the memory of Essex
> There's a tribute I must pay!
> So, the contents of this pot I shall
> Reveal this very day!
> (*Groans.*) Aaaaah!

(*BILL raises his head, struggles to arise, MONTE holds him, and SAUL rushes over to help MONTE, the former holding BILL's head down, the latter sitting on his back, during:*)

CHORUS. (*As VIOLET lurches from view.*)
> Bravo, Bessie!
> You'll bring it off somehow!
> Though it's troublesome—
> The time has come—
> To grin—and—bear—it—*now*...!

VIOLET. (*Off.*) Aaaaah!

PHYLLIS. (*Off.*) OH, dear!

GERRY. (*Turns toward audience.*) Is there a *doctor* in the house?

MONTE. (*Springs to his feet.*) I'm a doctor! (*Heads for UR archway, even as:*)

OTHERS ONSTAGE. You *are*—?!

MONTE. (*Stops just short of exit, making a sweeping gesture encompassing stage.*) You think I could make my living doing *this*?! Get real! (*Exits R, fast.*)

VIOLET. (*Off.*) Aaaaaaaah!

BILL. (*Starting to crawl UR.*) Violet! Violet!

SAUL. You mean, "Gillyflower! Gillyflower!,"
remember?!

BILL. *Violet*—!

SAUL. He's crazed with fatherhood!

GERRY. Why, Lord Essex, you're not as dead as we
thought! Who would have imagined— (*A large groan from
VIOLET, offstage.*) Oh, the hell with it! (*GERRY exits R,
fast.*)

PHYLLIS. (*Off.*) Shouldn't somebody be boiling *water,*
or something?

MONTE. (*Off.*) It's *beyond* that point!

BILL. (*Now moving in a fast scurry on hands and
knees, so fast that SAUL topples off his back.*) Violet!
Hang on! I'm coming! (*Scurries off UR.*)

LOUISE. (*Trying to make in-character small talk.*) *My*
but the kingdom's in for a surprise!

SAUL. That little dickens, *keeping* it from people!

LOUISE. She's had quite a day! Ascended to the throne,
defeated the Spanish navy, and produced a *new* heir to the
throne for the Big Finish! (*Offstage, we suddenly hear
BABY CRYING for a few moments.*)

AGGIE. (*Pops out from L behind-the-dais position,
heads off L, on:*) Don't mind me, folks, I'm just the royal
harpsichordist!

LOUISE. But where are you *going*?

AGGIE. (*Off.*) I'm bringing my *car* around to the stage
door! *Bill's* in no shape to drive!

POLLY. Frankly, Henry, *I* don't remember *any* of this!

HENRY. *Whaaat*—?

GERRY. (*Hurries onstage via UR archway.*) The new
heir to the throne of England will be passing through here

in a minute! And the *midwife* has some *birth* announcements for you!

PHYLLIS. (*Enters R, with several sheets of paper in hand, "disguised" by wearing Raleigh's cloak and hat; she passes these out to OTHERS onstage during:*) Here you are, loyal subjects! By royal command, we are all to *celebrate* the first viewing of the new heir in *song*!

SAUL. What *tune*?

GERRY. (*Aside.*) Same as the *old* finale!

LOUISE. But who's going to *accompany* us? The—uh—royal harpsichordist is—uh—bringing around the royal coach!

MONTE. (*Pops in UR.*) *I* will! I took piano lessons back in Barcelona! (*Drops from view to get at piano.*)

GERRY. Places, everybody! Here comes the happy couple and the new heir to the throne! (*LOUISE, GERRY, SAUL, PHYLLIS, and a very bewildered POLLY and HENRY, new lyrics in hand, assemble facing us from foot of dais, and:*)

LOUISE. Hit it, Don Diego! (*MUSIC INTROS, and:*)

CHORUS. (*Sings, still to "CAMPTOWN RACES" tune of original finale:*)

> Though Queen Bess insisted on
> Less sex, Essex
> Told her, "Single life's no fun!
> Let's be a pair!"

(*BILL enters UR, carry a bundled-up VIOLET in his arms, followed by a smiling SMITTY carrying "baby" wrapped in trailing executioner-cloak; they will cross briskly toward eventual DL exit, during:*)

'Cause if she didn't share,
The royal line stopped there!
So, he insisted they should have a *son*—

*(CHORUS points toward departing group, and SMITTY
pauses long enough to hold "baby" up to the audience
view for a second, on:)*

That's why she gave him ... the *heir*...!

*(CHORUS waves happily at departing group, which exits
as MUSIC ENDS; then CHORUS bows toward
audience, all grinning happily, and as they come up
from bòw, MONTE races around R side of dais and D
beside them, and:)*

MONTE. *(Has been looking at wristwatch again, now
points to it, on:)* And ... *Time!* We made it!
  GERRY. I thought the *lights* would go off at the
climax...?
  LOUISE. Monte thought a *slow fade-out* would be
more impressive, so that's what I programmed. *(LIGHTS
WILL START TO DIM DOWN, now, going FULL
BLACK on HENRY's line.)*
  PHYLLIS. Well, Monte, we've just set England back
about four-hundred years!
  MONTE. It's all right, Aunt Phyllis. Things were
merrier then!
  GERRY. Oh, but Phyllis—after *this* disaster, how can
you ever *hope* to get into the Bess Boosters?!
  LOUISE. Yeah, by *now* they've probably all taken
shotguns to their TVs!

PHYLLIS. Oh, who *cares* about that silly society! The only reason I got involved with them at *all* is so that I could get that *ten thousand bucks* for a group of people whom I love more than anyone in the whole wide world!

SAUL. Phyllis Montague—I could *kiss* you!

PHYLLIS. Saul Watson—who's *stopping* you?! (*They go into clinch, while OTHERS whistle/applaud in appreciation during:*)

MONTE. (*Heads DL.*) Now, excuse me, *I've* got to catch up with *Smitty!* (*Rubs his hands together in gleeful anticipation.*) A doctor's work is never done! *Wheeee!* (*As he exits:*)

POLLY. (*Wistfully.*) Henry, I *still* can't figure out what *scene* this is!

HENRY. *Whaaat*—? (*And there is a conclusive MUSIC-TAG as:*)

THE CURTAIN FALLS

End of Show

[NOTE: The preceding ending will *not* work to maximal effect if your lighting-tech doesn't have a dim-down capability; a blackout that goes from full lights to instant darkness on HENRY's line will be too jarring and abrupt for the audience. Therefore, if you can not provide that *slow fade-out* as indicated following LOUISE's line, *don't* end the show with HENRY's line, but continue onward thusly:]

SAUL. (*Breaks from clinch with PHYLLIS.*) Polly— Henry—the show is *over!*

POLLY. (*Cups ear; to SAUL:*) *Whaaat*—?
ALL EXCEPT POLLY AND HENRY. (*As loud as possible.*) THE SHOW ... IS *O-VER!*
POLLY. (*Smiles in pleased relief.*) Oh, good.
HENRY. (*A snarl of relief.*) And about time, too!

(Instant BLACKOUT and MUSIC-TAG as:)

THE CURTAIN FALLS

End of Show

IF YOUR STAGE HAS NO CURTAIN...

... run the show as indicated to your INTERMISSION; *have* your INTERMISSION; then, when your audience has returned, *before* you start Act II, insert *this:*

(AGGIE and LOUISE [in costume except for her hat] enter from RC area, toting gold-painted "throne" between them; "throne" will have a "WET PAINT" sign dangling just beneath front underlip of seat [but see note below]; during their dialogue, BILL and SAUL [both in costume, but SAUL minus any cloak or Shakespeare-wig or hat] will bring on U "flat" from UR and joggle it into place, somehow; this flat also has a "WET PAINT" sign at its center.)

AGGIE. Boy, with the *weight* of this thing, it *could* be solid gold!

LOUISE. It's made of mahogany. Mahogany's so heavy it won't even *float!* (*They will struggle throne up onto dais, during:*)

AGGIE. I sure hope this cockamamie dais can *support* the stupid thing!

LOUISE. Well, it's too late to worry about that *now!* But I'm *sure* it's not heavy enough to crush the *piano!*

AGGIE. It's an awfully *small* piano...! (*BILL and SAUL will enter here with UC flat.*)

LOUISE. You're just nervous because you'll be *sitting* at the piano!

AGGIE. Wouldn't *you* be?!

(In silence, now, they will move folding-chair aside, set throne where it should be, collapse folding-chair and take it down stairs of dais, during:)

BILL. This thing's too wobbly. If somebody *exhales* too hard it'll fall right over!

SAUL. It'll be okay once we get the *other* two wall-pieces attached to it!

BILL. But will it stay standing while we go *get* the other pieces?!

SAUL. Let's step away and see ...

(BOTH release flat, take mutual steps back from it, eyeing it nervously; it remains in place [flat should have L-shaped two-by-four "footing" on its hidden side for support]; BOTH blow out breaths in relief.)

BILL. So far, so good! Let's get the other flats, quick! *(Starts striding off R.)*

SAUL *(Hurrying after him on tiptoe.)* Tiptoe, *tiptoe!* *(BILL downshifts to tiptoe, and BOTH exit R on:)* And while you're at it, keep your fingers crossed! *(Even as MEN exit, just about the time when WOMEN have gotten down to foot of dais with folding-chair, SMITTY [minus wig/crown, but otherwise in costume] enters with taboret, music-box on taboret.)*

SMITTY. You forgot *this!* How *could* you forget this?! Where am I supposed to put anything *down* if you don't have *this* next to the throne?!

AGGIE. Give us *time*, will you?! This stuff's just gotten *dry!* It's not the end of the world!

SMITTY. *(Sincerely.)* It's close *enough!*

LOUISE. Oh, give me that, "your majesty," and go get your wig on! (*BILL and SAUL will enter R, toting what will be UL flat, and will get it in place and hooked to U flat, during:*)

SMITTY. (*Fingertips to hair.*) My wig! My crown! I forgot all about them! (*Rushes off in a dither, exits on:*) Where did I *put* them?!

LOUISE. (*Business of getting taboret in place beside throne.*) I can tell this is gonna be a fun evening!

AGGIE. (*Moving toward MEN.*) Easy, guys, you'll chip the paint! (*Will assist them in getting it hooked up [if this flat will have a continuing wall attached to its L side going straight downstage, have this piece "hinged in place" already; same goes for the other segment of wall that will shortly be positioned]; this flat also has "WET PAINT" sign on it.*)

BILL. Aggie, I have *better* things to worry about right now!

SAUL. Besides, once *Polly* gets onstage, nobody'll be able to *see* the walls!

GERRY. (*Rushes on DL in street clothes, will rush U and off UL during:*) What *time* is it? The stupid *car* wouldn't start, and then I remembered I'd forgotten my *costume* when I *did* get halfway here, and I was halfway *home* again when I remembered that the costume was *here* in the *dressing-room*, and—! (*She is off and gone.*)

LOUISE. (*Has started cross toward RC on GERRY's entrance, and now exits RC with folding chair, calling GERRY-ward over her shoulder as she vanishes:*) Well, as long as you're taking it *calmly*...!

BILL. (*Second flat is anchored.*) There! Come on, let's get the *other* one!

SAUL. Right! (*SAUL and BILL dash off, no longer tiptoeing, via RC; AGGIE removes sign from both flats over her speech:*)

AGGIE. Don't *run* with it! Take your time, guys! We have at *least* six minutes before the *curtain* goes up!... I hope.

VIOLET. (*Enters DL in street clothes, walking very carefully.*) Hi, Aggie. How's everything going? (*VIOLET will make her way toward UR, slowly, during:*)

AGGIE. About as *usual.*

VIOLET. *That* bad?

AGGIE. Actually, a little *worse:* Ordinarily, we could *delay* the curtain till we got everything set up, but with that TV-hookup timed to the second, we *have* to start on time, whether the set's in place or *not!*... Say, how are you *feeling,* Violet—?

VIOLET. Kind of tired. I had no *idea* a little *baby* could be so *heavy!* My lower back feels like I'm carrying a solid concrete *beach ball* up front! (*Exits UR.*)

AGGIE. (*Calls after her.*) Well, for heaven's sake, *sit down* somewhere!... If you can find a spot where you'll be safe from galloping farthingales! (*Looks around uncertainly.*) That's funny ... seems to me there was *one more* sign someplace—?!

NOTE: You now have *three options* with regard to that "WET PAINT" sign under the throne; do whichever you like, with your author's blessing:

OPTION #1

AGGIE. (*Cont.*) Oh, *there* it is! (*Removes sign from throne, and scene continues as written.*)

OPTION #2

AGGIE. (*Cont.*) Oh, well, maybe I miscounted. (*So she does not remove sign, and it remains in place throughout show.*)

OPTION #3

[For *this* version, the sign is in place but *unseen* because it's been swung up against the underside of seat, and will not come into view *until*, in the midst of "CHICKEN COQUETTE," *after* SMITTY has done her "sidesaddle" bit on the throne (during which she can *release* U end of sign, which will swing down but remain hidden by her skirt until she leaves dais), so that sign will *then* be revealed the first time she descends from throne, and of course ALL ONSTAGE CAN *REACT* TO ITS PRESENCE then, but be helpless to *do* anything about it since their show's in progress, and it will remain in view till end of show; if *this* is the version you do, AGGIE's line is:]

AGGIE. It's the oddest thing ... I'm *sure* there was another sign someplace ... but *where*?! (*Then she shrugs and dismisses it from her mind, alas.*)

[Your author must admit, version #3 is his personal favorite! But now, on with this pre-Act-Two insertion:]

(BILL, SAUL and LOUISE enter RC with final flat [which does not have a "WET PAINT" sign on it] and struggle to hook it into place, during:)

BILL. Come on, come *on*, the audience will be here any minute—!

SAUL. What's your hurry? It's not as though you knew your *lines, anyhow!*

LOUISE. Look who's talking!

AGGIE. *(Moving off R with signs.)* Is everybody *here* yet? I've been too busy to count noses. *(Exits R.)*

SAUL. *(Calls after her.)* I haven't seen anything of *Phyllis* yet—!

BILL. Count your blessings!

PHYLLIS. *(Off.)* Yoo-hoooo—!

SAUL. Too late!

PHYLLIS. *(Enters DL, all dolled up in a splendiferous outfit for the occasion.)* Isn't this too exciting for *words*?

SAUL. Apparently not!

PHYLLIS. *(Uncertainly.)* What—?

LOUISE. *(Quickly.)* Phyllis, why don't you go back and make sure Violet is taking it easy, okay?

PHYLLIS. Oh, dear, of course I will! How is she feeling? *(Will start UR during:)*

VIOLET. *(Off, shouts.)* Like Woody Allen [or Pinky Lee or Pee Wee Herman or any other notable of diminutive structure] playing *piggyback* with a *sumo* wrestler!

PHYLLIS. *(To LOUISE, in confidential tone:)* Is that good—?

BILL. *(Jaw-dropped.)* Are you *serious*?!

SAUL. Is she ever anything *else*?

PHYLLIS. What—?

LOUISE. *Go,* Phyllis, *go!*
PHYLLIS. Oh, very well! (*Exits UR.*)
BILL. (*Stands back to survey set.*) Well, what do you think?
SAUL. It'll have to do.
LOUISE. *That's* for sure! Excuse me, I've got to finish my *makeup*——!

[Go to BLACKOUT here, and pick up with GERRY's line, in darkness, that kicks off ACT TWO, Scene One; NOTE: If any other Elizabethan stuff is wanted on the set, it can be brought on during all the foregoing by MONTE or HENRY, sans dialogue, and placed wherever it goes—a shield on one wall, crossed swords on another wall, one of those hatrack-shaped supports from which a flag (a *modern-day* British Flag would be a real hoot) hangs fully open but sideways, etc. But do *not* have *POLLY* appear until her stuck-in-the-archway entrance, lest keen-eyed audience-members will *anticipate* her upcoming size-problem and spoil the joke. In re that joke: If you can work it, it would be funny if the UR archway were *hinged,* and when POLLY cannot go *through* it, she swings it downstage, enters *around* it, and moves down toward dais, with SAUL frantically "covering up" by shoving it back into place; do *not* have her move it again, however, since *repeats* of the gag won't be funny; have her subsequent entrances/exits be in that *sidle* through the archway. One last thing: If/Since you will be doing this show *without* a proscenium curtain, do PHYLLIS's before-the-curtain speech in a tight pin-spot light, with all the "behind-the-curtain" urgings at her simply coming out of the *darkness* upstage of her. References here, and throughout the show, to your "curtain" can be left *unaltered;* your audiences *knows* you have no curtain, but—trust me—they will accept any references to it regardless. Now—go knock 'em dead!

RICK ABBOT]

PRODUCTION NOTES

OFFSTAGE VOICES: The author has on occasion noted to his dismay, most especially during productions of *Play On!* the companion-piece to this show, that players take the indication "off" *literally* when speaking for the audience while not in view onstage. They seem to have forgotten that theatre design is aimed to *muffle* sounds from the wings; indeed, something shouted offstage *left* tends simply to proceed across the stage and offstage *right*, barely audible to the audience. Since the conversations and commentaries taking place in this show and its earlier companion are *vital* to the plot and the comedy, people offstage with lines should be speaking into a *microphone* with speakers concealed someplace *on*stage, so that the audience catches every last line from them. The same goes, in this show, for all *sound-effects* (excepting that in-full-view bit with POLLY's Velcro); for optimum effect, these should be heard *clearly*. So please, use speakers.

COSTUMING: Except where otherwise specified, the Elizabethan outfits are of the styles of those times— women with those farthingales extending their hip-lines sideways, floor-length gowns with high ruffs at the back on the neck, and a lot of sparkle and pizazz to the fabrics and accompanying jewelry; men in tights over which are worn those peculiar balloony shorts with vertical slashes, capes (short or long) on all shoulders, and doublets (sort of like vests with flared-out bottoms continuing slightly below the waistlines) and—where appropriate—hats with jaunty plumes. LOUISE, as the messenger, should be in a *man's* garb, and definitely wearing a plumed hat, with a moustache (but fooling *nobody*).

SEXES: When casting this show, Gerry, Louise and Aggie *can* be (with certain changes in pronouns in the dialogue) Jerry, Louie and Algie (addressed by Phyllis as Jerome, Louis [Loo-wiss] and Algernon). Of course, Gerry's role will *still* play a lady-in-waiting, so a "Jerry" will have to play this in drag.

PROGRAM: If you *do* opt for a program-*within*-the-program for "CHICKEN COQUETTE," although naming their show in print will kill the laugh when Phyllis reveals its name to the troupe, you should list Musical Numbers by (not cited in the script) *Phyllis's* titles for them; following the OVERTURE, the names of these songs are, in order of performance: HAIL, ELIZABETH!... LAMENT ... THE THRONE IS RIGHTLY MINE! ... I DREAM OF QUEEN E .... THOUGH YOU SHOULD DIE ... ALAS, ESSEX!... PAUSE FOR REFLECTION ...   AS I DREAM OF DEAR LORD ESSEX ... and FINALE. Don't forget to credit Saul and Henry for their *extra* roles in the show, but do *not* credit Violet (unless as something like "Production Assistant") as the substitute Elizabeth, of course. If you want, in the *real* program, you might want to list "Baby Essex courtesy of Coleco's Cabbage Patch Dolls" or whatever "baby" you decide to utilize.

VOCALIZING: By the very nature of this show, you can easily see that your players need *not* be trained singers, just able to carry a tune. If they *have* glorious voices, fine; but if they *haven't*, they'll fit this show's ambience like a glove.

DAIS: If a spinet-high level is too hard to manage, simply have the dais located in *front* of the spinet, with a "back wall" of the dais serving to conceal the spinet and its occupant (or occupants) on the bench from view.

WALLS: For *best* effect, these should be 5/8 of an *octagon,* rather than square-cornered; in other words, L and R walls should be at right angles to the front edge of the stage, the UC wall should be parallel to the front edge of the stage, and the two remaining wall-segments containing those *archways* should link these three other walls at 45-degree *angles* in UL and UR corners. But if your stage (or your budget) cannot manage them thus, the usual three-walled set will be perfectly acceptable, with the archways at L and R positions in the U wall.

THE BEEPER: You're naturally wondering why Louise, when adjusting Polly's Velcro does not take this golden opportunity to forestall the upcoming misplacement of sound-effects by Polly. Your author's thinking is that Louise has by now resigned herself to the fact that there is *no* way to salvage matters by now, and that trying to "fix" Polly's erroneous timing might only make things worse; this "thought-processes-of-Louise" is, of course, devilishly hard to *convey* to the audience without interrupting events for a pre-taped here-is-what-Louise-is-thinking bit to come over the speakers, an interruption with no comic payoff, alas, which would only serve to impede the show's progress. *BUT*—if this lapse really rankles with you, well—okay, here's something you can (at the discretion of your director) do at this point: Louise knows the beeper is in the farthingale, and that the next cue after the Velcro-bit is Smitty's "Be still, my heart!", which will bring on that unfortunate "COO-KOO" sound-effect *if* Polly's finger gets to the beeper-button, right? So: The moment Smitty says her line, and Polly's finger plunges toward that hidden button—have Louise *grab* Polly's wrist, have OTHERS all *freeze* in position, holding their breaths, watching intently,

have a determined Polly *slowly fight Louise's grip*, with
the irresistible strength of a determined combatant in
"Indian Wrestling," and despite Louise eventually using
both hands to stop that descending wrist, a determined
Polly *does* get her finger to the button, the "COO-KOO"
sounds, Louise releases Polly and gives a broad palms-
upward *shrug* toward OTHERS in a well-I-*tried* stance, at
which gesture OTHERS all release pent-up breaths in a
unified sigh of despair, and Bill can fatalistically proceed
with his "I bring you a gift ..." line, and the show can then
go on as written to its hopeless finish. The key to the
laughter here will be that group-*freeze* and the panting
breaths of Louise and Polly filling the resultant void,
puffing away in the ensuing silence ... and then it's COO-
KOO, shrug, unified sigh, and onward toward their mutual
doom. Got that? Good. And you are promised that, if done
right, this bit will get laughter *and* applause.

Also by
Rick Abbott...

Allocating Annie

Beauty and the Beast. Really.

The Bride of Brackenloch! A
Ghastly Gothic Thriller

But Why Bump off Barnaby?

Class Musical!

Dracula! The Musical?

June Groom

Play On!

A Turn for the Nurse

Please visit our website **samuelfrench.com** for complete
descriptions and licensing information.